BLACK WILLOWS

JILL HAND

Black Rose Writing | Texas

ISBN: 978-1-68433-586-2
PUBLISHED BY BLACK ROSE WRITING
www.blackrosewriting.com

Printed in the United States of America
Suggested Retail Price (SRP) $17.95

Black Willows is printed in Calluna

*As a planet-friendly publisher, Black Rose Writing does its best to eliminate unnecessary waste to reduce paper usage and energy costs, while never compromising the reading experience. As a result, the final word count vs. page count may not meet common expectations.

To Henry, who encouraged me to tell stories.

BLACK WILLOWS

PROLOGUE

In another life he'd been mean as a rattlesnake with a sore tooth. His name – Dorje – meant thunderbolt. Those who tangled with him came to regret it.

Now Dorje Rinpoche, former loan shark, extortionist, general badass and currently the leader of a spiritual community, sat in the lotus position on a woven wool prayer mat in the temple's main shrine room. The mat depicted a graceful pair of red-crowned cranes hovering over Mount Meru, the sacred five-peaked center of the universe in Buddhist philosophy. The rinpoche's eyes were closed, his hands loosely clasped in the lap of his maroon robe.

A breeze drifted through the bamboo slats of the louvered windows, bringing with it the scent of rain and sweetly fragrant jasmine. It stirred the colorful silk appliqué *tson-tang* thangkas on the walls. The cloth rippled, causing intricate circular mandalas and eight-spoked wheels of dharma to flutter as the storm drew near.

Cones of sandalwood incense sent up tendrils of smoke before a ten-foot-high gilded bronze statue of Amitābha, the Buddha of infinite light. There was a deep rumble of thunder and the rain intensified, drumming furiously against the red and gold clay tiles of the temple's roof. The rinpoche sat unmoving, as still as the statue towering over him.

At the back of the room a nun stood, patiently waiting for the rinpoche to end his mediation. From the passageway behind her came the patter of bare feet and the sound of murmured conversation as monks departed the dining hall after their simple midday meal.

Finally, the rinpoche rose in a single fluid movement. He was in his seventies, his face fissured with wrinkles, yet he moved with the graceful athleticism of a young man.

"I have considered your request," he told the nun. "Do you insist on going through with it?

"I do," the nun said. "We tried everything in our power to banish the creature. Nothing worked. We need help."

"Then go, you have my blessing."

CHAPTER ONE – DIOPTASE

The helicopter flew toward an emerald-green oval rising from the clear blue water of the Aegean Sea. At sixty-eight acres, Kardos wasn't the largest of the islands of the Cyclades archipelago. Neither was it the smallest. In the opinion of Aimee von Helgern, who was thinking of buying it, Kardos was just right, like Baby Bear's chair, porridge, and bed, in the story of Goldilocks and the Three Bears.

The island's owner was an American actor named Axel Moorlock. He had fallen prey to a Ponzi scheme which swept through Hollywood like a tornado, decimating fortunes and leaving its victims stunned and incredulous. On screen, Moorlock was famous for portraying diabolical villains, but in real life he was trusting as a newborn lamb. He'd put his faith in a slick-talking investment counselor who promised to quadruple his money then skedaddled with his ill-gotten gains to parts unknown. Thus, Moorlock was forced to sell Kardos, as well as the house in Malibu.

"Dioptase," said Aimee, looking out of the helicopter window at the shimmering blue water below.

Celena Drakos raised a carefully groomed eyebrow. "I beg your pardon?" Celena was a sleek Athenian, a member of the Hellenic Association of Realtors. The two women sat facing each other in supremely comfortable white leather seats. Pink-tinged lightbulbs set into the burled oak paneling above their heads gave a soft, flattering glow to their faces. This was no ordinary chopper but one manufactured by the Italian company Leonardo for its luxury division. Among its customers were shipping magnates, movie stars, heads of state, and televangelists. The latter chose to ignore what Jesus said in Luke 18:22, opting instead to accumulate all the loot they could while they were alive and phooey to whatever might come later.

"Dioptase," Aimee repeated. "That's what the water down there reminds me of."

"What is that, exactly?"

"It's a copper cyclosilicate mineral, emerald-green to bluish-green in color. It's sometimes found in quartz. Its luster is vitreous to sub-adamantine."

Celena found that not only incomprehensible but mind-numbingly boring. Nonetheless, she widened her eyes, pretending to be riveted. "How fascinating," she said.

"I became interested in minerals and gemstones after my husband gave me a necklace with a four-hundred-and-eight-carat green diamond known as the Imperial Chameleon. He said it reminded him of the color of my eyes." Aimee met Celena's gaze with eyes that were the pale, witchy green of absinthe. "Naturally occurring green diamonds are rare. The Imperial Chameleon is even rarer because it changes color. I started collecting gems and reading up on minerals. People are wrong when they say the Aegean is the color of turquoise. It's like dioptase in quartz."

"That's absolutely..." Celena tried to think of another word for 'fascinating,' since she'd already used that one. Her English vocabulary was good, so she was able to come up with an appropriate substitute. "Enthralling," she said. That's absolutely enthralling."

If Aimee had compared the Aegean's color to that of spaghetti sauce, Celena would have enthusiastically agreed. A sizeable commission was riding on this.

Aimee stretched her long legs in slim-fitting black trousers. Her white t-shirt stopped six inches short of the waistband of her trousers, giving a view of her taut abdomen. Printed on the front was ENDANGERED? WHO CARES? Beneath was the image of a mouse-like creature called a lesser Thorndyke's shrew. It was native to Sri Lanka, where it was threatened by habitat loss. The shrew's face wore a piteous expression, as if it suspected it was doomed.

The shirt was one of Aimee's designs. She was CEO and chief designer of Clobber, a clothing line known for its use of provocative slogans and images.

"Almost there," said the helicopter's pilot. He was a handsome Greek with a thick black mustache and intensely white teeth. Mirrored aviator shades hid his eyes, but judging by his appreciative smile as he turned his head to glance at Aimee, he found her good to look upon.

"Kardos is only ten minutes from downtown Athens by helicopter, thirty-five by speedboat. The island is both secluded and convenient to a vibrant nightlife, as well as sophisticated cultural, shopping, entertainment and dining experiences," Celena said, quoting from the sales brochure.

"That's great. Are there any snakes?"

"Yes, in the main house. I notified the housekeeper to have them ready."

"Are there a lot of different kinds?"

"I'm sure there are."

"Good. I have a large collection back home in New York. I keep them in an apartment across the hall from the one where I live."

Celena was flummoxed. "A separate apartment for your snacks?" She was aware that the ultra-wealthy were prone toward indulging their eccentricities, but she'd never heard of anything like this. Perhaps Aimee had an eating disorder? That could explain why she had an entire apartment devoted to snacks. Aimee was greyhound-thin, as elegant as a Ming vase, but that didn't necessarily mean anything. Thin people could have eating disorders.

"Snakes, not snacks. My goodness! What would I do with an apartment full of snacks?" Aimee laughed. "I have dozens of snakes. They're housed in their appropriate habitats, each with its own correct climate. I had large glass cases built for them, backed with paintings made by the son of the man who painted the dioramas for the Academy of Natural Science in Philadelphia. A herpetologist lives on site to care for them. I have spared no expense as to their comfort." She smiled dreamily. "I have dozens and dozens of snakes, and I love every one of them."

"How delightful," said Celena, who could hardly bear to think of dozens of snakes living in an apartment. "Then you're in luck. There are leopard snakes on Kardos. We Greeks call them *ochentri,* meaning viper, but they are not venomous."

"That's too bad. I like venomous snakes. Any others?"

Celena thought about it. "I think also on Kardos you will find what are called cat snakes. They are venomous, but their venom is too weak to hurt anyone, even small children. They feed on lizards, spitting the venom and using it to stun them."

"I'd like to see that," said Aimee.

The helicopter banked as it passed over a grove of olive trees. It touched down with a gentle bump. Aimee and Celena unbuckled their seat belts. "We'll be back in about an hour," Celena told the pilot.

"Isn't he coming with us?" Aimee asked. Before Celena could answer, Aimee addressed the pilot. "Come with us. You'll be bored waiting here by yourself."

He looked to Celena, as if asking for permission. "Yes, come with us," she said.

They climbed down onto the helipad, the pilot gallantly taking Aimee's arm. The sunlight was pure and clear, the air pleasantly warm, scented with lavender and thyme. "I am Stavros," the pilot said, folding his sunglasses and tucking them in the front pocket of his shirt. The first two buttons were unbuttoned, black hairs springing up around the links of the thick gold chain around his neck. "Welcome to Kardos. It is a beautiful island for a beautiful lady such as yourself."

"This is a nice place," said Aimee, looking around. "And you," she said to Stavros, swatting him lightly on the arm, "are a big old flirt. They told me to watch out for Greek men."

"We Greeks are poets at heart. When we are in the presence of beauty, we must pay homage to it. It is the Greek way." Stavros flashed his white smile and squeezed Aimee's arm.

Celena cleared her throat. "Let's get on with it, shall we?" She gestured to an ugly building made of stone the color of orange sherbet. Its curving lines and horseshoe arches made it resemble a hybrid of Arabian Nights palace and art deco toaster. "Ahead is the main house, Pathanos Villa. It is absolutely stunning, inside and out, recently refurbished to the highest of standards."

Their footsteps crunched on the white marble chips of a walkway lined with cone-shaped junipers as Celena continued her spiel. "Pathanos Villa sits on a headland, with the sea on both sides. The sandy beaches, perfect for swimming, snorkeling or just relaxing, provide a stunning view of magical sunsets. This is truly a paradise on earth, removed from the stresses of everyday life. The estate has its own vegetable garden where grapes, pomegranates, melon, watermelon, strawberries, limes, peppers, chilies, tomatoes, and much more are plentiful."

"Pomegranates are the most Greek of all fruit," Stavros confided to Aimee, leaning over to murmur in her ear. "You are perhaps familiar with the legend of Persephone. Hades, smitten by her loveliness, bore her away to the Underworld, where she ate pomegranate seeds." He squeezed her hand and drew her closer to him.

"Stavros," said Celena pointedly. "Why don't you go tell the housekeeper that we're here?"

He gave Aimee's hand a final squeeze before sauntering away.

"Honestly," said Celena, shaking her head. "To continue, over there are the guest cottages. There are four. The largest can be divided into two separate units should the need arise. Each cottage has its own plunge pool and private balcony. Over that way are the tennis courts. Over there is the putting green. Every amenity you could possibly want is here: wine cellar, staff quarters, exercise room, a movie theater which seats thirty-five, a state-of-the-art security system and much more."

They passed by a swimming pool which gave off a pungent smell of chlorine before entering the coolness of the house. "I direct your attention to the mosaic on the floor of the foyer. It came from an ancient villa on Crete," said Celena.

Aimee regarded the brightly colored tiles beneath her feet with a frown. "The guy with the pitchfork in the chariot pulled by weird green things. Who's he?"

"The ancient Greeks called him Poseidon. He was the god of the sea." Celena didn't correct Aimee by telling her the three-pronged object Poseidon held was a trident, not a pitchfork, and that the weird green things – half-horse, half-fish – were called *hippokampos*.

Americans, she thought dismissively. But if Aimee bought the island, Celena couldn't care less if she didn't know a trident from a socket wrench.

After a lunch of grape leaves stuffed with rice and ground beef, grilled octopus, olives, cheese and baklava, they continued their tour. Aimee found the property to her liking. "The asking price is thirty-five million euros, right?" she asked Celena. That's, what? About thirty-nine million dollars?"

"Thirty-eight million, seven hundred and eighty-eight thousand."

"I'll pay thirty-six million, as long as all the furnishings and all the appliances and everything else you showed me are included, especially the popcorn maker in the movie theater; I really like that."

The amount Aimee named was precisely the lowest price the seller was willing to accept. He hadn't said anything about the popcorn maker being part of the deal, but Celena doubted it would be a problem. She readjusted her opinion of Aimee. She might have as about as much knowledge of Greek mythology as a sea cucumber, but she had excellent business sense.

"I'll inform the seller of your offer and get back to you," she said.

Stavros sidled up to Aimee. "You will be happy here," he purred. "You and your husband."

"Actually, I'm a widow. My husband passed away not long ago. It was quite sudden."

Aimee thought it best not to mention that her husband had been stabbed to death by her father's butler, in her family's mausoleum, no less. That was too bizarre for public dissemination.

"I am sorry to hear it," Stavros said. "A beautiful lady like you needs a husband to lavish her with affection. Perhaps you will find another husband, or a very good friend. Perhaps you will find one here, in Greece." He looked at her meaningfully.

"Who knows?" said Aimee.

To Celena she said, "I'll call my banker as soon as I get back to my hotel. It's only seven o'clock in the morning there, but I'll call him at home and let you know what he says. It shouldn't be a problem."

Ninety minutes later, a hotel chambermaid pushing a cart filled with linens past the closed door of Aimee's suite heard an anguished cry from within, followed by a *thump* as something struck the wall. It was Aimee's cell phone, which she flung after getting bad news from her banker.

"Dammit!" she screamed. "I can't believe it."

CHAPTER TWO - THE HO CHI MINH TRAIL

Marsh Trapnell and his nephew Benjamin Monteleone were walking around the quarter-mile track at Rayburn Academy, a boarding school for boys in the Allegheny Mountains of Pennsylvania.

The track was a gift to the school by the parents of one of the graduates, who went on to win a silver medal in the Olympics for the hundred-meter dash. The track's springy green polyurethane surface gave pleasantly beneath the soles of Benjamin's scuffed sneakers and Marsh's John Lobb wingtips, which had been polished to a mirror-like shine.

It was a splendid autumn day, the mountain air crisp and invigorating, the leaves on the trees ablaze with orange and yellow and crimson. Marsh was enjoying himself. Benjamin was not.

Benjamin had been "stuck twenty" in the argot of Rayburn, where he was a member of the junior class. That meant he'd been given twenty demerits as punishment for leaving the school grounds without permission. One of the teachers had spotted him downtown in front of the Starbucks, drinking from a large container of coffee. Coffee was forbidden to the boys at Rayburn, although the staff could have as much as they liked. Most of them indulged themselves copiously from the coffeepot kept constantly topped up in the teachers' lounge. The more heartless among them liked to lecture to their classes with a steaming mug of coffee in hand.

Boys stuck with demerits had two choices: they could circle the track once for every five demerits, or they could work off their punishment by reporting to the head groundskeeper and pull weeds, rake leaves, empty trash cans or do whatever else needed doing. The head groundskeeper, a grizzled curmudgeon named Ricky Stumpf, loathed the boys at Rayburn, considering them to be a bunch of pampered, insufferable brats. That's why most of them, including Benjamin, chose to walk off their penalty on the track. In the parlance of Rayburn it was known as walking the Ho Chi Minh Trail.

Benjamin asked his uncle what that meant. "Things here have special names. Dessert is 'boss.' Freshmen are 'worms.' Dances with the girls from Pettigrew are called 'pig scrambles,' which is really mean. I hope the girls don't know."

The Pettigrew School was a nearby girls' boarding school. The girls there were aware of the demeaning term, having been gleefully informed of it by their brothers and male cousins. In return, the Pettigrew girls referred to dances at Rayburn as 'freak shows at Pimple McNerd Academy.'

"The Ho Chi Minh Trail was a military supply route running from North Vietnam through Laos and Cambodia to South Vietnam, during the Vietnam War," Marsh told Benjamin. He bent down to remove an oak leaf which had plastered itself to the toe of his shoe. "Do you know about the Vietnam War?"

Benjamin made a face. "I'm not stupid."

"I never said you were. The Ho Chi Minh Trail was used to send weapons, manpower, ammunition and other supplies from communist-led North Vietnam to their supporters in South Vietnam. I can only surmise that the track began being called that by boys who went to school here during that time."

"Makes sense," said Benjamin.

They passed the field house. On the roof, painted in red, was GO RAYBURN RAMS! They kept walking. Two circuits completed, two to go. Benjamin was starving. He'd skipped lunch so he could eat in town with his uncle, but they couldn't go until he finished his laps.

Lunch in town was a prized event for Rayburn boys. The food at school ranged from mediocre to downright awful, unless the board of trustees was meeting. Then the dining hall was transformed as if by magic. Flower arrangements and starched linen tablecloths appeared on the tables and prime rib was served instead of sloppy joes or tuna-noodle casserole.

"Take the quadrangle between the administration building and the library. You said it's called Long Acre Square. That's what Times Square was known as before the *New York Times* moved there shortly after the turn of the twentieth century," Marsh said. "This school was founded in the eighteen-eighties, 1 believe. With old institutions like this, things tend to take on special names that get passed down through the years."

At eighteen Benjamin was old to be admitted to Rayburn, especially since he was able to produce only a few patchy records to show that he'd ever attended any other schools. The headmaster made an exemption in his case and let him in anyway. Exemptions were sometimes made for certain boys, particularly when, like Benjamin, an influential alumnus spoke up for them.

The truth was Benjamin was quite intelligent, but his formal education had been astonishingly spotty. Although he spoke five languages and was a whiz at math, he was ignorant of many major events in American history. He was hazy on how many states there were, for instance. He was unable to name the three branches of the federal government, much less describe their functions. Moreover, he'd never heard of many well-known works of literature, once innocently asking if *The Great Gatsby* was an autobiography written by someone named Gatsby.

Benjamin was far from the densest student at Rayburn Academy. That dubious honor belonged to a Senator's son named Tyler Cottrell. Tyler once inquired in biology class whether penguins were fish or birds.

"1 don't see what you guys think is so funny. Fish swim. Penguins swim. Why wouldn't they be fish?" he complained as his classmates whooped with laughter.

Tyler's parents had sent him to Rayburn when he was fourteen, hoping the school could drum some sense into him. He was now twenty, tall and broad-shouldered, with thighs like tree trunks. He was strong as an ox and not much smarter than one. By the look of things, Tyler might still be enrolled at Rayburn when he was thirty, either that or be given some kind of sinecure position there.

A stocky boy approached Marsh and Benjamin as they trudged along the track. He wore grey sweatpants and a crimson hoodie with a big white R on the front, representing the school colors of red and white.

The boy hailed Benjamin manfully. "Yo, Monteleone! You going to the pep rally tonight?"

"I'll be there," said Benjamin. "Uncle Marsh, this is Clayton Weber. He's the head cheerleader. Clay, this is my uncle, Marsh Trapnell."

"Oh, wow," said Clayton. "I thought he was your dad, the count. It's a pleasure to meet you, sir."

He stuck out his hand for Marsh to shake.

"The pleasure is mine," Marsh said, shaking hands. "Male cheerleaders are a venerable tradition. They go back to the early days of football at Ivy League universities like Harvard and Yale. I'm pleased to see Rayburn is continuing it."

"It ain't like there any chicks here to go out for cheer," said Clayton. He thrust a hand in the pocket of his sweatpants and fished around, coming up with a piece of purple bubble gum. He removed its waxed paper wrapper, popped it in his mouth and chewed briskly. "Not that chicks would be anything more than eye candy. Men make awesome cheerleaders. Me and my boys holler our asses off. We do, like, six backflips in a row and shit." He punctuated that statement by blowing a bubble.

"Impressive," said Marsh. "I salute your dedication to school spirit."

"Thanks," said Clayton. He surveyed Marsh's navy-blue double-breasted merino wool suit. Although Marsh was no larger than a jockey, there was something about his air of unruffled poise coupled with his perfectly turned-out appearance that hinted at formidable capability.

"The reason I thought you were Monteleone's old man was because of your suit. That's Italian tailoring, if I ain't mistaken," Clayton said.

"It is indeed," Marsh said, adjusting the knot in his tie. "The designer's name is Enzo D'Orsi."

"I heard of him. Some of his suits go for sixty grand. That's baller! When I make my first million I'm gonna dress sharp, not like my old man. He buys his suits off the rack from Emil's Big and Tall Business and Formalwear. They look like dog shit."

Clayton nodded respectfully to Marsh. "Stay fresh, my brotha," he told Benjamin. The two of them performed a complicated handshake. It was something the boys at Rayburn invented, hoping it made them seem like gangstas.

"What an interesting young man," said Marsh, watching as Clayton swaggered away. "And what a colorful vocabulary!"

"He toned it down some because of you. You should hear him in the dorm. Every other word out of his mouth is muthafuka."

"I'm glad I won't have the opportunity," said Marsh. "Foul language has its place, but its frequent use in casual conversation indicates a less-than-stellar intellect."

As they completed lap three, Marsh asked, "Speaking of your father, have you heard from him lately?"

Benjamin's father, Count Benedetto Francesco Guillermo d'Olficcio de Monteleone, was a knitwear designer. He and Benjamin's mother were divorced. The count lived in Rome, with his new wife and infant son.

"Not lately, no. He's probably forgotten I exist."

"Your mother hasn't forgotten about you. The last time we spoke she told me all about her visit with you on Homecoming Weekend."

"I know," Benjamin said, smiling. "When the guys in my dorm saw her picture in my room, I think they started counting the hours until she got here. One of them went, 'I didn't know your mom was Aimee Trapnell, the fashion designer. No disrespect, Monteleone, but she's hotter than hell's hibachi.' "

Aimee used her maiden name for her fashion business. In her personal life she used the surname of her late second husband, Franz-Albert von Helgern.

Benjamin and Marsh started in on lap four.

"Do you like it here?" Marsh asked. "Special Agent Burns thought you would."

Carson Burns was an FBI agent with whom Marsh had formed a reluctant alliance. In lieu of being sent to prison for a variety of misdeeds that might have put him behind bars for the rest of his natural life, Marsh had been given the opportunity to report what he knew about even worse miscreants to the FBI. Agent Burns was his "handler." Their relationship had grown from mutual dislike to grudging acceptance after Marsh saved the world from destruction by preventing a nuclear weapon from being dropped into a volcano.

Agent Burns' father was the first black student admitted to Rayburn Academy. He went on to become a professor of political science at Georgetown University and an assistant Secretary of State. Agent Burns thought her father's old prep school was the right sort of place for Benjamin.

"I do like it here, actually. I didn't think I would at first, but it grows on you," Benjamin said.

Two boys ran whooping through a pile of leaves, pursued by a golden retriever, its tongue lolling. The boy in the lead tauntingly waved a knitted hat. "Give it back, O'Keefe!" the other boy shouted.

"Stuff like that, normal stuff," Benjamin said, jerking his chin at the boys, who had reached the theater building and vanished around its corner, followed by the dog. "I never had that before. It's nice knowing what to expect. Every morning at seven a worm knocks on my door and goes, 'first bell for breakfast!' Then I know I can turn over and sleep for another fifteen minutes or get dressed and be one of the first ones in the dining hall. The whole day goes like that, one thing after another, predictable, you know? Before, I had tutors, or when I went to an actual school we kept moving around so much for Mom's business that I never finished a year at any school I went to. I went to a lot of schools in New York, London, Milan, Antwerp, Tokyo, Dubai. I don't even remember the names of some of them. Then I stopped going and well..." He looked away, chewing on his lip.

"You ended up addicted to drugs, hanging out with street kids in Amsterdam and getting a tattoo on your wrist that says 'pickled squid meat' in Chinese Han characters. Followed by a stint in rehab. I imagine Rayburn Academy would be a refreshing change after that," Marsh said dryly.

"I'd like to kick that tattoo guy's ass," Benjamin fumed. "Every time somebody asks me what my tat says I feel like getting on a plane, flying over there, and punching him in the nose for pulling a dirty trick like that on me."

"I doubt he knew what it says. He probably saw it written down somewhere and liked the way the characters look," Marsh said.

His cell phone rang. He looked at the screen. "It's your mother," he told Benjamin.

"Hello, Aimee," he said. "You'll never guess where I am."

"I don't give a shit where you are. Something horrible has happened."

"Mom?" said Benjamin worriedly. He could hear his mother's panicked voice coming through the phone's speaker. She sounded as if she'd been swept up in some kind of terrifying natural disaster.

"I'm at Rayburn Academy with Benjamin," Marsh said. "Aimee, are you all right? What's going on?"

"Oh, god! I can't believe it! It's awful, just awful," she wailed.

"Aimee, where are you? What's going on?" Marsh asked, prepared to drop everything and rush to her rescue. Was she ill? Kidnapped? Whatever was wrong, she seemed to be in desperate straits.

"I'm in Greece. I've had the worst news. I can't buy an island I want. It has a beautiful house on it, and there are snakes there, but that bastard Holt Whittaker at the bank said I don't have enough money. How can I not have enough money?" Aimee's voice rose incredulously. "This has never happened to me before. Before, whenever I wanted something, I went ahead and bought it. Now Whittaker says I can't buy the island, or I can but I shouldn't because it would mean I have to sell some of my stocks or cash in some bonds before they mature and I'll get hit with a huge penalty. I don't like this. I don't like it at all."

"Your mom's all right, she's just having a little bit of a financial issue, nothing for you to worry about," Marsh told Benjamin.

Benjamin's dark eyebrows drew together. "Can I talk to her?"

Marsh passed him the phone.

"Hi, Mom. Is everything okay?"

"It's fine, darling. Just a little fuss with my banker in Atlanta. Silly Mister Whittaker says I can't buy an island. I'm going to go see him and make him understand that I *need* that island. I'm sure he'll apologize and let me have the money."

"You don't need it. Nobody needs an island; you want it. There's a difference."

"No there's not," said Aimee. "If I want something I have to have it, but let's not argue, sweetie. How are things at school?"

"They're good. I'm on the lacrosse team, and Monsieur Legrand asked me to tutor some kids who need help in French."

"Marvelous, darling! I have to go. My flight's boarding. I'm on my way to Atlanta. I'll stop in and see your Uncle Trainor and Aunt Palmer while I'm there. Bye-bye!"

The call ended.

"She's on her way to Atlanta to talk to her banker. Some guy named Whittaker," Benjamin told Marsh.

Marsh sighed. "Poor fellow. He has no idea what's about to befall him. Your mother in the mood she's in right now isn't going to be particularly nice for Atlanta. They'd probably prefer a visit from William Tecumseh Sherman and his troops."

Benjamin thought for a moment. "Civil War, right?"

"Correct! Good, Benjamin, you're learning American history. Bravo! Now it appears we've walked the Ho Chi Minh Trail the requisite four times. Let's go sign you out and we'll have lunch. I passed a cozy little bistro called Stumpy's Diner on the way here. It had a certain rustic charm. I hope you had a tetanus shot recently."

He took one look at Benjamin's horrified expression and burst out laughing. "I'm joking! We'll go to that place you like, the one with the *prix fixe* menu, how's that?"

CHAPTER THREE – ICEBERG RIGHT AHEAD!

"And then," Palmer Trapnell told an architect named Chase Merriweather, "An alarm will sound, one of those that goes *aoogah! aoogah!* The room will start filling up with ice-cold water and everyone will have to swim to safety. What do you think of that?

Merriweather looked over Palmer's shoulder to where her husband stood. Trainor Trapnell was shaking his head and frantically waving his hands, as if to say, No way! That's insane!

"Well," the architect said cautiously. "It's an interesting concept."

"I know! Escape rooms are popular right now. My friend Chandler Woodbury has one. It's at Lakeland Mall, between Razzle-Dazzle Doughnuts and Sweet and Sassy Lingerie, where that store that sold things like blacklight posters and lava lamps used to be. You have to find clues to figure out how to escape from a room done up like a library in a spooky old mansion. *This* will be much better."

Palmer beamed complacently. Her sandy blonde hair was cut in an asymmetrical style popularized by an actress with a starring role in a daytime television drama. Palmer was a former dog groomer who had advanced several rungs up the social ladder by marrying Trainor. With her bright pink lipstick and Lilly Pulitzer twin set, she was the apotheosis of an affluent young Atlanta matron.

Palmer and Chandler Woodbury, ostensibly friends, were locked in a mortal combat of one-upmanship. If Chandler had an escape room, then Palmer wanted a better one.

"But the logistics," Trainor said desperately. He drew up a chair and seated himself next to his wife at the polished mahogany conference table in Merriweather's office. He spread his hands in mute appeal to the architect to put an end to this nonsense. "That's what they're called, right? Logistics?

Ways of doin' things? You can't fill up a room up with water and make people swim out. It's not safe. What if somebody drowns? And how do you empty the water out afterwards? I don't see it."

He turned to Palmer, who had folded her arms across her chest and was pouting. "I'm sorry, Chicken Legs, but I think it might be illegal."

Chicken Legs was Trainor's his pet name for his wife. When she was in a good mood, she called him Boo Bear. She was not in a good mood at the moment. She snapped, "Trainor Scott Trapnell, you took a solemn vow when we stood up in church in front of all our friends and family and Reverend Batts joined us in holy matrimony. You promised to make me happy. Having this escape room will make me happy. You can't go, 'What if somebody drowns? And 'It might not be legal.' You have to be on my side here and get me my *Titanic*-themed escape room. You *have* to."

"Tell her, Chase," Trainor implored the architect. "Tell her it won't work."

Merriweather drummed his fingers on the table, lips pursed. "It might work," he said, earning an appalled look from Trainor.

"See, I told you," Palmer gloated.

Merriweather stood up. He passed in front of the brass sign on one of the conference room's silvery gray walls which said 'Aaronson & Merriweather, Architectural Design.' His hands clasped behind his back, he looked out of the floor-to-ceiling window onto traffic moving below on Ponce de Leon Avenue. The faint blatting of car horns drifted up to the fourth floor of the Tupelo Building, home to Aaronson & Merriweather.

"Yes, I think it might work, with certain modifications."

"Like what?" Palmer asked suspiciously.

"Flooding the room is out, for one thing. It's too dangerous. You'd have to carry a cripplingly huge amount of insurance and require participants to sign a waiver releasing you from liability in case anything went wrong. Even then I don't think you'd get it approved."

"But that's the best part!" Palmer wailed. "How can it be like being on the *Titanic* if there's no water coming in?"

"Fifteen hundred people died when the *Titanic* sank, little bitty kids, some of them. I read about it online. It would be in bad taste to recreate it. Honest, Chicken Legs, it would," Trainor pleaded.

"I disagree. I think it would be an exciting experience," Palmer said. "We could give out certificates saying 'I survived the sinking of the *Titanic.*'Sell t-shirts, too. We could sell all sorts of things . People would line up for miles to get in."

"You're not thinking of making a full-size replica, are you?" Merriweather asked.

"I don't see why not."

"For one thing, the cost would be prohibitive to build a ship as long as three football fields. For another you wouldn't need all those staterooms or an engine room or coal bunkers and some of the other things they had on there."

"I guess not," Palmer said reluctantly. "We probably don't have to have coal bunkers."

"I assume you want it to be free-standing, so it looks like the *Titanic*, with a black hull, white superstructure, and four buff-colored smokestacks. I suggest making the hull out of fiberglass instead of steel. Nobody will be able to tell the difference." Merriweather was busily jotting down notes as he spoke. "I think we can make this come together for you. We've got a relationship with a firm of engineers. One of them used to work in the design department of a theme park I'm not going to name, but I'm certain you've heard of it. He can recreate a safe, educational, *respectful* experience, at, say, one-quarter the size of the *Titanic.* It would have all the sounds of an ocean liner of that era: the ship's horn blasting, engines making whatever sounds the engines made, cries of seagulls, ship's bells, and so on. He can even rig it so the floor moves, duplicating the pitch and roll of the ocean. It can have the scent of salt air piped in, everything done perfectly to duplicate the feel of being on board."

Trainor couldn't believe his ears. "Free-standing? Can't you just put it in one of the empty stores at a mall, the way Chandler Woodbury did? Holy cow, how much is this thing gonna cost?"

"That's not important," Palmer told him. "What's important is giving people the opportunity to find out what it was like on board the most famous ship in the world. It will be elegant and thrilling. I'm gonna have beautiful gowns and hats made up for the women I hire to play the female passengers, and tuxedoes for the men. They'll mingle graciously with the guests and there'll be musicians playing violins and a beautiful staircase just like in the movie. It will be incredible."

"What about hitting the iceberg?" Trainor asked. "And sinking?"

Palmer waved a French-manicured hand. "I'm sure they can find a way to make it shake so it feels like it hit the iceberg. People won't have to climb into lifeboats that get lowered into the water, if that's too dangerous. We'll have an old man with white hair and a white beard dress up like the captain. He'll come out and go, 'Sorry, folks, but we hit an iceberg and we're sinking. I must stay and go down with the ship, in the tradition of the sea. The rest of you, get into the lifeboats, women and children first.' Then they'll line up and get into cars that look like lifeboats and down a ramp they'll go, safe and sound. Elegance, that's the thing. Recreating a bygone era. This is gonna be great, Boo Bear! Say we can do it, please?"

Trainor sighed. "All right, why not? It's only money. Who knows? This thing may even turn a profit. I'll put in a call to Holt Whittaker at the bank and let him know."

Palmer squealed and threw her arms around him. Merriweather applauded. "You won't be sorry," he said. "I'll start making calls and putting together preliminary sketches."

CHAPTER FOUR – DRIP AND SPLASH

The day after he and Palmer met with the architect about Palmer's plans to recreate the *Titanic,* Trainor stood atop a stepladder, wrestling with a large oil painting. The painting hung on the wall of a room known as the Gentlemen's Parlor in Trainor's ancestral home, White Oaks plantation. Sweat beaded his forehead as he struggled to free the painting.

Standing below him, nervously wringing his hands was Lee Gi-yong, the butler at White Oaks.

"Sir? Mister Trainor, sir? Are you sure you want to do that? Shouldn't I get a couple of the gardeners to lift that down for you?" Lee asked.

"I don't want them messin' with this. I got it; it's just a little heavy, is all. Oof!"

The hooks holding the steel cables on the back of painting to a metal rail bolted to the ancient plaster wall suddenly came free. Trainor flinched and jerked out of the way as the cables whipped around his head. He swayed precariously, holding onto the painting.

"Oh, sir! Please be careful!" Lee cried.

At the last moment, when it seemed certain he would fall, Trainor regained his balance. He climbed down the ladder, clutching the painting and breathing hard. "Piece of cake," he panted. "Help me get this wrapped up, would you? The, uh, appraiser over in Mobile wants to have a look at it, and at some of these other ones Daddy bought. For insurance purposes, you understand."

"Yes, sir," the butler said.

Seeing them standing side-by-side there was a marked contrast between the two men. Lee was slim and clean-shaven, his straight black hair neatly trimmed. He wore his usual informal work attire of navy blue jacket, white shirt, plaid bow tie and crisply pressed chino trousers. Trainor, on the other hand, might have been a time traveler from the Summer of Love. Bearded and shaggy-haired, he was clad in faded denim cutoff shorts and bright yellow rubber flip-flops. A Hawaiian shirt emblazoned with scowling tiki masks strained to button across his belly.

"I thought your father's art collection had already been appraised," said Lee.

"Yeah, but that was years ago. These things have to be updated on a regular basis. Now go get me some bubble wrap and duct tape, okay?"

"Certainly, sir," the butler said. He left the room, but not before casting an admiring glance over the artwork on the walls. There were two Hockneys, a Picasso, a nude by Modigliani, a Lichtenstein, and a Motherwell. There was also an amusing piece by Claes Oldenburg consisting of a burlap chicken feed sack stuffed full of pink rubber gloves, the kind used for washing dishes. The Gentlemen's Parlor was an Aladdin's cave of priceless twentieth-century art. It was only a tiny portion of the collection assembled by Trainor's late father, Blanton Trapnell, most of which was on loan to museums.

Palmer came in carrying a plastic shopping bag. "I got the paints," she said, shaking the bag. "The canvases are in the car. Where's Jubilee?"

Jubilee was Palmer and Trainor's seven-year-old daughter.

"She's out back, playin' with Seamus," Trainor said, referring to his late father's Irish setter.

Palmer studied the painting Trainor had taken down from the wall. It was propped up against a black leather-upholstered Le Corbusier sofa, waiting to be encased in bubble wrap and carted off to Mobile.

White Oaks was completed in 1831, rising from mosquito-infested swampland like something from a fever dream. Its galleries with their lacy wrought ironwork shaped like vines and flowers echoed those of the fashionable French Quarter in New Orleans. The original blueprints called for the plantation house to have twenty rooms, including a ballroom with metal springs beneath its floor and walls covered in mirrors that somehow contrived to make the persons reflected in them appear more attractive than they actually were. More rooms were added in the ensuing centuries. The current number was around forty, although none of the Trapnells had ever troubled to take an exact count.

The Gentlemen's Parlor had initially been furnished with gorgeous inlaid and gilded walnut and tulipwood pieces purchased at bargain prices in France in the aftermath of the Revolution. The room had stayed that way, frozen in time, until Blanton inherited the house. Then he'd redecorated, consigning what he called "old junk" – some of it made expressly for Marie Antoinette by master cabinetmakers Jean-Henri Riesener and Georges Jacob – to the rubbish heap. Now the Gentlemen's Parlor was a sterile testament to the mid-twentieth-century-modern aesthetic, all chrome and smoked glass and kidney-shaped tables.

"Lord almighty, that'll be easy to copy. It doesn't even look like anything," Palmer said, referring to the original Jackson Pollock propped against the couch. Blanton bought it in 1950, sight unseen, after reading an article about the artist in a magazine. "I'll tell Jubilee to dribble paint all sloppy-like on the big canvas I got that's the same size. Nobody will be able to tell the difference."

Trainor had lied to Lee about having some of the paintings in his father's collection appraised. In reality, he intended to have Jubilee make copies and sell them as originals. That he actually believed a seven-year-old child would be able to produce a forgery convincing enough to fool anyone other than a complete idiot was a sign of his desperation. Palmer's *Titanic* project was going to cost upwards of twenty million dollars. Trainor didn't have that much money. His banker had told him so.

There was the sound of the heavy front door slamming, followed by a rapid clicking of heels across the black-and-white marble tiles of the entry hall. Then Trainor's sister Aimee appeared in the doorway.

"Are y'all opening up an art-supply store? There's about ten blank canvases stacked up in the back of the BMW out front," she said, laughing. Then she caught sight of the Pollack leaning against the sofa.

"How come you took that down?"

Palmer and Trainer exchanged glances. "We're takin' it to be appraised," Trainor said, running a hand nervously through his shoulder-length hair.

"Taking it where?" Aimee asked suspiciously.

"Mobile. See, the appraiser's in Mobile. He said to bring it on over and he'd, um, update the assessment. We gotta do it for insurance purposes," Trainor said, repeating the lie he'd told Lee.

Smelling a rat, Aimee put her hands on her hips and glowered at him. "What kind of art appraiser makes you bring a valuable painting like that to him? They come to you when you've got a museum-quality collection like Daddy's. I think you're bullshitting me, Trainor. I think you're taking that painting to your scuzzy pal Peach Walker to sell. He lives in Mobile, him and his criminal mama."

"Peach Walker is my very dear friend," Trainor said with dignity. "I won't have you callin' him scuzzy."

"He *is* scuzzy," Aimee replied. "He and his mama run a crime syndicate. That moving and storage company of theirs is a front for all sorts of crime. If something's against the law, you can bet Peach and his mama are up to their necks in it. You and Peach got Benjamin mixed up in that business that got my husband murdered and lost us the best butler we ever had. We'll never find anyone half as good at running this house as Hillman was. Hello, Lee."

That last was addressed to Lee Gi-yong, who had returned unnoticed, carrying rolls of bubble wrap and duct tape. Pretending he hadn't heard what Aimee said implying that his performance was inferior to his predecessor's he addressed Trainor. "Here are the packing materials you wanted."

To Aimee, he said, "Good afternoon, Ms. von Helgern. It's a lovely day isn't it?"

"It is if you consider one-hundred-degree heat and ninety percent humidity lovely."

"It *is* a bit warm, isn't it? We're fortunate this old place has such effective air conditioning," said Lee, who was no stranger to heat and humidity. He'd previously worked in Washington, D.C., in the embassy belonging to the Republic of Korea. If the Trapnells didn't pay him double what he made there, he would turn right around and go back. He'd never met anyone quite like the Trapnells before. There was something reckless and dangerously self-serving about the entire family, as if they might take it into their heads at any moment to embark on some horrendously ill-advised project and force him to participate.

There was a silence. Finally Lee got the hint. "May I bring everyone a cold drink? There's fresh lemonade and sweet tea."

"How about mint juleps?" Palmer said.

"Yes! That would be just the thing," said Aimee. "You know how to make a mint julep, don't you, Lee?"

"Of course," he said stiffly.

"Then use the sterling silver and pewter julep cups. They're on the top shelf of the breakfront in the dining room, behind the big cut-glass punchbowl. You'll have to take the punchbowl down to get at the julep cups. Watch out; it's heavy. You'll have to take the punch cups down, too. There are one hundred of them. They belonged to my great-grandmother Eliza Culpepper. They were presented to her along with the punchbowl in appreciation for her work with the United Daughters of the Confederacy. You might be interested to know that during the war her mother found a man hiding in her barn, some dirt-poor cracker who refused to fight for the Confederacy. She beat him half to death for his cowardice with a cast-iron frying pan, can you imagine?"

"Yes," said Lee, who could easily imagine Aimee beating someone with a frying pan.

"Count the punch cups to make sure none are missing and look them over to see if any are chipped. The last time we used them was for the open house after Daddy's funeral. People aren't as careful with other people's things as they are with their own."

"Yes, ma'am," said Lee, suspecting there was more.

"Serve the mint juleps on the silver tray Daddy got from the Elks Club for being man of the year. I don't think we used it lately, so it might need polishing. And don't forget to muddle the mint. You can cut some that's growing out back in the herb garden."

Aimee glanced at Palmer and Trainor. The unspoken message was clear: *There, that should keep him occupied.*

When Lee left the room Aimee turned angrily to her brother and sister-in-law. "You're trying to sell that painting. Don't lie; I know what you're up to. You were going to sneak behind my back and sell it and keep the money for yourselves. You got Peach Walker to line up some kind of, I don't know, Russian oligarch or Mexican drug lord to buy it, didn't you?"

"He's not Mexican. He's Colombian," Trainor said defensively.

"Oh my god," said Aimee, smacking her palm against her forehead. "You know that's illegal, don't you? Stealing a painting and selling it to a drug lord? I presume he's paying cash, cash that he got from selling drugs. That is *so* incredibly illegal! You've got plenty of money from your trust fund. What could you possibly need that made you think it would be okay to do that?"

"It's not stealing. Daddy always said I could have any of these pictures in here that I wanted. He told me so, Aimee, yes, yes he did," Trainor said as his sister shook her head in vigorous denial. "And I'm not selling any to no drug lord, so there. Now that Daddy's dead I don't see any reason why I can't go ahead and…"

"Shut up, Trainor," said Palmer.

In a conciliatory tone she told Aimee, "With your daddy's will not being able to be probated because they can't locate Karen we didn't think it would matter if we raised some money by doing a little business with people Peach knows."

Karen was Aimee and Trainor and Marsh's half-sister, their father's daughter by his first wife. He had named her executor of his will, but she could not be located. Without her the will could not be submitted for probate. A judge was deciding how to proceed. What the judge didn't know – what no one knew, except for Aimee and Marsh and Trainor – was that Karen was dead.

"Why?" Aimee asked. "What's the hurry? Why not wait? Daddy's will is going to be settled, eventually. It's in the safe in his office. We know what it says. He left everything to his children to be shared equally, so why sneak off behind my back and get Peach Walker involved? Nothing good ever happens when Peach Walker gets involved. Please explain, because I'm at a loss here."

"I want to build the *Titanic.* I got a site all picked out for it," said Palmer.

Aimee stared at her. "You can't be serious."

"I am totally serious," Palmer said hotly. "It's going to be an escape room, only better because it will be educational. It'll be a tribute to a more gracious age, before people went around dressed any old sloppy way."

Palmer's own husband frequently went around looking like he just rolled out of bed. She'd long ago given up on attempting to turn Trainor into the sort of neatly groomed, impeccably attired mate she'd always hoped for.

"Chandler Woodbury has an escape room. I want one, too," Palmer said.

"I should have known. First Peach Walker and now Chandler Woodbury. They're both awful. Yes, they are," Aimee said when Trainor and Palmer started to protest. "Those canvases in the car, let me guess. You were going to try and forge the Pollack and some of these other paintings, weren't you?"

"No we weren't," Trainor said.

"That's a relief. For a minute there I thought…"

Palmer interrupted her. "We were going to get Jubilee to do it."

Aimee sank into an egg-shaped chair, stunned speechless.

"Jubilee is very talented, artistically," Palmer said. "Her teacher said so. At parents' night she said Jubilee was the best artist in the whole second grade, didn't she, Trainor?"

"That's right," Trainor said. "And since Jubilee is so good at art, we thought it wouldn't hurt to have her copy a few of these paintings. Not forge, copy," he said quickly when Aimee opened her mouth to protest. "There's a difference."

"No there isn't, not if you intend to pass them off as the real thing. I can't believe this. This is crazy, even for you. Experts have ways of telling how old paint is, and canvases. Putting aside the fact that you're involving a child in art forgery, one look at whatever you had Jubilee paint and they could tell right away it's not an original."

"Like that one," said Palmer, pointing to a painting of a black dog hanging on the wall. Both its eyes were on the same side of its head. It was looking at a bird with stick-figure legs.

"Yes, like that," said Aimee, glancing at the familiar painting she'd seen every day of her life while she was growing up. "Exactly. Anyone can tell it's genuine."

Trainor snickered.

"What?" said Aimee. "What's so funny?"

"Look in that cabinet over there."

He pointed to a birch storage cabinet designed by Finnish architect Eliel Saarinen. Inside Aimee found a painting of a black dog sitting on its haunches. Both its eyes were on the same side of its head. Its head was cocked, studying a bird with stick-figure legs. Astonished, she looked from the painting in the cabinet to the one on the wall. They were identical, down to the underlined signature carelessly dashed across the bottom: Picasso.

"See?" crowed Trainor. "See, I told you. Your little niece is a darned good artist."

CHAPTER FIVE – MONSTER HEAD

Trainor and Palmer's scheme was both bold and foolish. They planned to keep the original paintings and sell copies made by Jubilee. They figured Peach Walker could hook them up with plenty of shady characters eager to acquire valuable works of art, no questions asked.

"It's not like South American drug lords or Japanese yakuza are art experts. Give them a chance to buy a Picasso or any of these others in here that look like two blobs and a scribble and they'd be all over it like honey on a hot biscuit," Palmer said happily.

"That's right," Trainor agreed. "Daddy was a big art collector. He got wrote up in magazines all the time. If we tell some Russian gangster or some Mafia kingpin from New Jersey that a picture came from Daddy's collection they'll practically throw money at us. Guys like that don't know diddly about art."

"That may be, but they have people who do," Aimee told him. "Do you feel like getting your fingers cut off when they find out they've been cheated?"

"We thought of that," Trainor said smugly. "We're not gonna tell them our real names. We're gonna use aliases. I'm Monsieur Loup-garou and Palmer's Madame Fifi Chanel."

Aimee shook her head, choosing not to comment on how ridiculous those names were. "Peach will tell them your real names. As soon as one of them complains that they got ripped off Peach won't only tell them who you are, he'll draw them a map showing how to get to your house."

Just then Jubilee scampered in, followed by Seamus. The dog's claws clicked on the polished parquet floor as he went from Trainor to Palmer to Aimee, hoping one of them would give him a treat, or a head-scratch. When no treats or head-scratches were forthcoming, he went into the entry hall and curled up in his basket to await further developments.

Jubilee was small for her age, pot-bellied and knock-kneed, with a snub nose and lank brown hair. Her eyes, however, were remarkable, the same pale green as Aimee's. None of the other Trapnell siblings had those eyes, nor did Aimee's son Benjamin. They were a genetic fluke, passed down from a long-forgotten Scottish ancestress. Like Aimee, this Scottish lady was a force to be reckoned with. She'd taken part in clan warfare, her long black hair streaming behind her as she rode through the night, gleefully anticipating the destruction about to be rained down upon her enemies.

As a child Aimee had been unattractive. She'd turned out to be a stunner. Palmer and Trainor hoped Jubilee would undergo the same metamorphosis.

Jubilee cupped something round in her hand. She covered it protectively with her other hand when she saw her mother looking at it.

"Don't put that nasty old tennis ball of Seamus' down on anything; it'll get it all dirty," said Palmer.

"I won't," said Jubilee. "Aunt Aimee, did you bring me a present?"

Aimee did not get up to hug or kiss her niece, nor did Jubilee expect her to. The Trapnells, as a rule, did not display physical affection toward one another. Aimee dug in her purse and came up with several little glass vials stamped with AIMEE TRAPNELL'S NIGHT GARDEN.

"Here you go," she said, handing them to Jubilee. "This is perfume, made just for me. It's not available for sale yet. You're the first one to have a sample, except for some of the people who work for me and several thousand fashion writers and bloggers and influencers. That makes you very special."

"Thanks," said Jubilee glumly, putting the samples in the pocket of her shorts. She didn't think much of it, in terms of a gift. A toy would have been better.

"Can I have one?" asked Palmer. "I want to show it to Chandler Woodbury. You don't have any full-size bottles, do you? That would really impress her."

"A one-ounce bottle retails for two hundred and fifty dollars," Aimee told her coldly.

"Well, surely you don't pay that much. All I'm asking for is one little bottle to show my friend, but if it's too much trouble…"

Jubilee reached in her pocket and handed her mother the samples. "Here, Mommy."

Palmer pulled Jubilee to her and hugged her violently. She glared over the child's head at her sister-in-law. "Thank you, Jubilee. What a generous little girl you are. You're not stingy one bit! Not like *some* people. Bless your sweet little heart!"

Jubilee's breath was knocked out of her by her mother's fervent embrace. The round object she'd been holding fell from her hand and hit the floor with a *thud.* It was not a tennis ball.

It rolled to where Trainor sat. He'd taken off his flip-flops and was swinging his legs, idly kicking the back of the Pollack with his bare toes.

He drew his feet up onto the sofa at the sight of the hideous object staring up at him. "What the fuck?" he gasped. It was a carved and painted wooden head with three bulging, lidless eyes, crowned by a row of human skulls. Its mouth was open to reveal pointed fangs. There was something deeply disturbing about it. None of the adults wanted to touch it. When Jubilee went to pick it up Palmer grabbed her by the arm.

"Don't! It might be dangerous."

"But I want it," Jubilee wailed. "It's mine. The lady gave it to me."

"What lady?" Aimee asked.

"The lady in the dinosaur plant house."

There were several large, domed conservatories in the gardens behind the house. One was devoted exclusively to ferns. Someone had given Jubilee a book about dinosaurs that named ferns as being among the plants they would have eaten (those that weren't meat-eaters.) Since then she always referred to that conservatory as the dinosaur plant house.

"Do we have a female gardener?" Palmer asked Trainor. "I thought all the gardeners here were men."

"How the hell would I know? Aimee, did Daddy hire any female gardeners?"

"I think he did have one a while back. She was an intern from the University of Georgia. I remember she asked Daddy for a letter of recommendation and he spelled her name wrong. He said in the letter that the university shouldn't let women major in landscape architecture. It should make them study home economics instead. You know how old-fashioned Daddy was. She emailed me about it, all upset. That was years ago, though. I don't think any of the gardeners here now are women."

Aimee looked at the wooden head with revulsion. Who would give such an ugly thing to a child?

"What did the lady look like?" she asked Jubilee.

"I don't know,"

"You must know. You saw her. She gave you a freaky wooden head. How old was she? What did she look like? Was she white or black? Come on, Jubilee! Think!"

Jubilee's lower lip quivered. "I don't know."

"Jesus, Aimee, you're scaring her. Don't interrogate her like that," Trainor said.

He got down on his knees in front of his daughter and put his hands on her shoulders. "Don't cry, honey. Aunt Aimee didn't mean to scare you. Tell me what the lady looked like. Was she younger than Mommy or older?"

"Older," Jubilee whispered.

"A lot older, or a little?"

"A lot."

Trainor looked up at Aimee triumphantly. "See? Now we're gettin' somewhere. Nice and easy, that's how to talk to kids, not like you're gonna smack them around."

He returned his attention to Jubilee. "Okay, so the lady was a lot older than Mommy. Was she the same color as Mommy, or was she the color of Louetta and Miss Sonya?"

Louetta was the cook at White Oaks. Miss Sonya was the music teacher at Jubilee's school.

Jubilee's forehead wrinkled in confusion. "What do you mean?"

"You must have noticed people have different skin colors. Was the lady black or white? Or was she the color of Lee? He's Asian. Asians are a different color than us. Don't tell me nobody ever explained this to you."

Jubilee blinked at him, uncomprehending.

Trainor turned to Palmer. "Can you believe this? Her school's too busy teaching them about butterflies and the environment to tell them people are different colors."

Turning back to Jubilee, he said, "Listen up: Miss Sonya is black. Louetta is black. Mommy is white. Got that?"

Jubilee began to cry. She sobbed, "Miss Sonya and Louetta aren't black; they're toasty brown. Mommy is brown, too; she's light brown."

"That's because Mommy goes outside and plays tennis and golf. If Mommy stayed inside all the time she'd be white like paper," Palmer told her.

"I don't want you to be white like paper. Nooooo!" Jubilee moaned.

"Well, this is fantastic. Way to go, you two," Aimee said. To Jubilee, she said, "Your mother's not going to turn white like paper. She was only fooling. What did the lady in the dinosaur plant house say to you? Anything? Or did she just hand you the monster head?"

Jubilee wiped her nose on the sleeve of her t-shirt on which cartoon rabbits cavorted, maniacal grins on their faces. "She said, 'Hi, Jubilee. Tell your Aunt Aimee I'll see her soon.' Then she gave me the monster head. Please can I keep it?"

CHAPTER SIX – STRANGER DANGER

Aimee was nonplussed. Who was this woman who had mentioned her by name, saying she'd see her soon? Aimee hadn't told anyone she was coming to White Oaks. It had been a spur-of-the-moment decision after she'd talked to her banker in Atlanta. He'd held firm on his opinion that she didn't have enough funds to buy the Greek island, not without dipping into her capital, which he strongly advised against. Discovering that her brother and his wife had received the same disappointing news and had gone to White Oaks, she'd driven down to Cobbs to join them. So how did this mysterious woman know she was there?

She must not have known, Aimee decided. She must be one of the ladies from town, perhaps Birdsall Gormley. Birdsall had been president of the Cobbs Garden Club for as long as anyone could remember. The garden club ladies sometimes came out to White Oaks and puttered around in the conservatories. It must be Birdsall Gormley, who was eighty-six and resembled an egret, all beaky nose and long, skinny legs. She'd been after Aimee to establish a work-study program for high school students in the gardens at White Oaks. No doubt that was what she wanted to see her about.

Why Birdsall Gormley would have given Jubilee a creepy wooden head was unknown. Perhaps she'd picked it up on one of her mission trips overseas with the First Baptist Church and thought the child would like it. You never knew with Birdsall; she was batty, like all the Gormleys.

"I'm going out there and talk to her," Aimee said. "I have a feeling it's one of the garden club ladies, probably Birdsall Gormley."

Trainor made a face. "Don't invite her in. We'll never get rid of her."

Birdsall was known for being talkative. An encounter with her at the post office or Buzzy's General Store could last an agonizing two hours, while she catalogued her ailments as well as those experienced by all her relatives, living and dead. Then she'd launch into soliloquies about the weather, the economy, and the state of affairs in Atlanta and Washington before declaring how young people nowadays have no manners. (She'd been saying the same thing for half a century.) Then she'd go into how nothing is built to last anymore, ticking off a list of every household appliance she'd purchased going back thirty years and how they'd all failed to live up to her expectations. By that time her captive listener would be woozy and despairing, swaying on their feet with boredom and feeling as though they might never escape her clutches.

That was why no one willingly sought out Birdsall Gormley's company without having an excuse prepared in advance which would allow them to get away: an urgent dental appointment, perhaps, or the sudden recollection that they'd left the stove on.

Trainor told Jubilee, "You shouldn't talk to strangers. They might do something to you. Didn't your teacher tell you about stranger danger?"

Jubilee shook her head. "No. What's that?"

Trainor looked at his wife. "I think we should consider sendin' her to another school. First, they don't tell kids how people come from different races and then we find out they don't tell them how strangers could do all kinds of horrible things to them. And not just strangers, anybody."

Jubilee gasped. "What?"

Trainor reconsidered. "Well, maybe not anybody, not your family, but other people you know might turn out to be secretly evil. They pretend to be nice at first, but then they get you alone and, oh boy! Before you know it you're handcuffed in a tumbledown old shack with a dirty sweat sock stuffed in your mouth while a fiend in human form fires up a chainsaw."

Jubilee's eyes widened. "What do they do with the chainsaw?"

Her father shook his head grimly. "I'm gettin' to that. Let me tell you what happened to a little girl once. She was about your age and she looked a lot like you. One day she was walkin' down the street when a man drove up. She'd seen him around town and he'd always been friendly so when he asked her to get in and help him look for his lost dog she didn't see any reason why she shouldn't..."

When Aimee returned a few minutes later Jubilee was sucking her thumb and staring blankly straight ahead, frightened out of her wits by the story her father made up to illustrate the concept of stranger danger.

"What's the matter with her?" Aimee asked.

"Beats me," said Trainor. "Did you see anybody out back?"

"Only two of the gardeners. I caught them sitting on a bench, loafing." She smiled, recalling how they'd leaped up at the sight of her, stammering that they'd been taking a short break. "They said they hadn't seen any old ladies, or any ladies. Whoever it was must have left."

The gardens at White Oaks were known far and wide for the variety of the specimens and the care taken with the plantings. Blanton Trapnell's mother Norma had expanded and improved upon White Oaks' original formal gardens after she made a 1912 visit to the newly opened Brooklyn Botanic Garden.

Norma didn't like to venture north of Richmond, Virginia, into what she thought of with fear and loathing as Yankeeland. However she'd been lured by the prospect of shopping on Fifth Avenue. She also wanted to see a Broadway play called "Within the Law." It was a thrilling melodrama starring her favorite actress, Jane Cowl. Norma would have liked a career on the stage, but propriety forbade it. She settled for living vicariously through the exploits of actresses like Cowl, who had large bovine eyes and a genteel little quaver in her voice that made it seem as if she was about to burst into tears at any moment.

After visiting the Brooklyn garden Norma decided she owed it to the South to make a better garden than the one the Olmstead brothers designed for the former rat-infested ash dump.

What she came up with was impressive. Besides the fern conservatory and the succulent and bromeliad conservatory there was one devoted exclusively to orchids. They made a spectacular display, ranging in color from ghostly white, to leopard-spotted, to purple, to red, to jet black, and from the size of a dime to that of a saucer. An artificial waterfall twenty feet high added to the dramatic setting as it tumbled over moss-covered rocks, sending up a filmy mist resembling a bridal veil. Laborers with pickaxes had dug the rocks from the banks of the Suwanee River and hauled them to White Oaks by mule-drawn wagon.

The humid atmosphere inside the glass dome and the thunder of the waterfall combined with the vibrant colors of the orchids to make it seem as if a piece of the Amazon rainforest had been plucked up and set down in South Georgia.

Outside the conservatories, spread across some sixty-eight acres, were a variety of features, including a boxwood maze and fountains that sent jets of water shooting high into the air. There were tulips and crocuses and daffodils in season, as well as some four thousand azaleas and an equal number of rhododendrons in shades ranging from white to delicate pink to vibrant red.

The gardens were a showplace, but their carefully tended perfection ended with an unruly tangle of hundreds of black willow trees marking the beginning of a swamp. Their leaves were yellow-green like those of weeping willows, but the bark on the trunks of the older trees was so dark a brown as to appear almost black.

The swamp went on for miles, smelling pungently of muddy, stagnant water and rotting vegetation. It was almost impenetrable, filled with cypress knees, water weeds and water oaks, their limbs draped with kudzu. Alligators and snakes and all kinds of bothersome insects made the swamp their home. Much of it had been deeded over to the state for use as a nature preserve. It was in this swamp that Karen, half-sister to Aimee and Trainor and Marsh had drowned.

Lee came in carrying the mint juleps on a tray. It had taken him a while to find the silver tray Aimee had requested, the one the Elks had given Blanton. He finally discovered it in the back of one of the shelves in the pantry, behind bags of dog food. He'd polished it then polished the mint julep cups. Then he'd counted all one hundred cut-glass punch cups, washed and dried them and put them back in the breakfront. He felt like some cursed character in a fairy tale, forced to attempt to perform an impossible task. Then he'd gone out to the herb garden and picked fresh stalks of mint.

That done, he set to preparing the mint juleps. He placed mint leaves in the bottom of the julep cups and poured sugar on top, mashing with a wooden muddler until the leaves began to break down, releasing their oil and tangy aroma. Then he poured bourbon whiskey over crushed ice, stirring until the cups were frosty. He added straws and fresh sprigs of mint for garnish. By this point, Lee had lost a good deal of his crispness. Sighing, he arranged the frosty cups on the tray. He forced himself to stand up straight with his shoulders back then he carried the tray and its cargo of beverages into the Gentlemen's Parlor.

"Finally! I thought we were going to die of thirst waiting for you," said Palmer.

"Sorry, ma'am," said Lee, thinking longingly of the job he'd left at the embassy. He held out the tray to her, and to Aimee and Trainor. Then he went over to Jubilee.

He gave her a big smile. "I have lemonade for you. It's in a pretty cup, like the ones your mommy and daddy and auntie have, but it's better because it's got a paper umbrella in it. I put it there especially for you. Later on I'll take you out back to the goldfish pond. We'll feed the fish together, just you and me and nobody else. What do you say to that?"

Jubilee shrieked and buried her face in her mother's lap.

They got her calmed down and sent her into the library where she had her own shelf with some children's books which had belonged to her father and his siblings. Lee kept asking what he'd said that had frightened her.

"Who knows? Don't worry about it," said Palmer.

CHAPTER SEVEN – ALBATROSS

The Trapnells drank mint juleps and considered how they could get the money they wanted. Aimee wasn't about to give up on her dream of acquiring an island she could fill with snakes. Palmer was determined to create a landlocked version of the *Titanic*. Trainor knew he had better go along with her or she'd make his life miserable.

To most people the siblings would seem fabulously wealthy. A trust fund set up by their late father made it so Trainor never had to work a day in his life. Aimee, who had more get-up-and-go than Trainor, used money from her trust fund to start Clobber, her fashion line. She chose the name for its double meaning, both to give someone or something a severe beating and Cockney slang for clothing and accessories.

Aimee had a lavish lifestyle, complete with a Lamborghini and not one but two apartments in the Dakota on Manhattan's plush Upper West Side.

Their brother Marsh had established himself as an international arms dealer. Marsh enjoyed the chaotic and dangerous nature of his chosen profession, which kept him constantly on his toes, always active, never bored. Unlike his siblings he didn't crave more money.

Despite all the luxuries they enjoyed, to Aimee and Trainor it felt like a horrible calamity that they couldn't afford to buy a Greek island or build a simulacrum of the *Titanic*. What were they going to do?

"All I needed was about forty million dollars," Aimee said morosely.

"My *Titanic* project would only cost about half that much. I don't see why Holt Whittaker can't let me have it. It's not that much money," said Palmer.

"It kinda is, Chicken Legs," Trainor said. "Twenty million dollars kinda is a lot of money."

"Not when you're gonna inherit twelve billion it isn't. Then twenty million is a drop in the bucket," said Palmer.

Trainor drained his drink. He placed the empty cup on the kidney-shaped Noguchi coffee table in front of the sofa where they sat side by side, the Pollock having been moved to make room.

"I see your point, honey," he told his wife. "I tried to convince Whittaker how this *Titanic* project is sure to be a big success. I asked him if he couldn't see his way clear to turn loose some of my money he's got invested, but it was no-go. He went on and on about how it would be bad for me to use my capital. He went, 'Don't eat your seed corn, son.' I didn't understand half of what he was sayin', but the part I did understand was that once Daddy's will is probated, we'll have plenty of money. We gotta talk to Judge Sparks again. Get him to get a move on. Seems like legal business takes forever."

Palmer perked up. "Good idea, Boo Bear. Get him to declare Karen dead and appoint another executor. How hard can that be?"

This line of conversation was making Aimee uncomfortable. She was aware that her stepsister was dead, having killed her. Aimee had seen Karen fall into the algae-covered brown water of the swamp behind White Oaks and not come up. She must still be down there.

Aimee sighed, exasperated. If she had it to do over again, she wouldn't have murdered Karen, but it seemed like a good idea at the time. Karen was nearly twenty years her senior. She had treated Aimee horribly when she was growing up, pinching and taunting her and once pushing her down the stairs, breaking her arm. Another time she had poured boiling water on Aimee's feet, claiming it was an accident.

Karen had established a school for girls in Nepal. Girls from impoverished families were given a smattering of instruction in reading, writing, and mathematics, but the bulk of their time was spent making handicrafts. The fruit of their labor was sold to stores throughout America, Europe, and Asia through a shell company called Himalayan Village Treasures.

Blanton donated a substantial amount of money over the years to Karen's pet project, the Dhaulagiri School for Girls. The last time he talked to Aimee about it, he claimed to be thinking of making Karen the main beneficiary of his estate, valued at around forty billion dollars.

He may not have meant it. He could have said it simply to make Aimee furious. There were few things Blanton enjoyed more, once all his former business rivals were either dead or driven into bankruptcy, than pitting his children against one another.

It was an entertainment he never tired of – letting the right hint drop, or dredging up a humiliating incident from the past – then sitting back and watching their reactions.

The conversation that sealed Karen's fate took place one afternoon when Aimee was in Cobbs for a visit. She and Blanton were in Blanton's office in White Oaks.

"It does my heart good to see you doing so well, honey," Blanton started out, smiling benignly at her from behind his battered metal desk. He had a sentimental attachment to that desk, due to it being a relic from an automobile dealership, the first business he ever owned outright.

"Thank you, Daddy," said Aimee. Her usual clipped transatlantic tones were elongated and softened until they practically dripped with molasses. It was how she always spoke when she was around her father, like she was Scarlett O'Hara and he was Daddy O'Hara, the two of them taking it easy on the old plantation.

"You've done all right for yourself," Blanton continued. "Married to a German nobleman, running a successful business. You deserve a pat on the back."

Blanton neglected to mention Aimee's son Benjamin, his eldest grandchild and formerly the apple of his eye. At that point Benjamin had dropped out of school and was a fixture in the coffee shops in Amsterdam's Red-Light district.

Aimee hoped her father's next words would be that he was going to do something special to demonstrate how proud he was of her, perhaps deed White Oaks over to her. Instead, what he said next made her blood run cold.

"Trainor and Marsh are established, Trainor with a fine little daughter." (Aimee gritted her teeth, thinking how Benjamin was worth ten of Jubilee, if he'd only straighten out.) "It's Karen I'm thinkin' of. Marsh is happy as a clam at high tide, sellin' weapons all around the world, but Karen is alone out there in Nepal. She never married and she's not gettin' any younger. To me, she's right up there with Mother Teresa, the way she's selflessly helpin' those poor children. Don't you agree?" He looked at her keenly, a slight smile on his face.

"Yes, Daddy," said Aimee. *You have got to be kidding,* she thought. *That so-called school is a sweatshop.*

"So maybe," said Blanton cheerfully, "maybe I ought to make a new will. You wouldn't mind, would you, honey?" He leaned back in his chair and smiled at her, an elderly shark sniffing the water for blood.

"No, Daddy. Of course I wouldn't mind," said Aimee, wanting to scream. "The only thing is, don't you think it's not good that Karen pays those little girls pennies a day to make necklaces and bracelets and things? Some of them are only eight years old."

"Pshaw! What nonsense! They're grateful for the opportunity. Why, when I was a boy during the Depression I picked cotton and was glad to do it."

He didn't add that he picked cotton on one of his father's farms for precisely one day, in order to learn how it was done. After that his father put him in charge. The rest of that harvest season Blanton sat on the porch, drinking iced tea and fanning himself with a Panama straw hat, drowsily watching the field workers as they moved through the rows of cotton.

"Yes sir, those were hard times, brutally hard times. Plenty of people died, times were so hard, but I made it through," Blanton said reminiscently. He'd been a freshman at the University of Georgia back then and drove a snazzy, brand-new Packard two-door roadster. "It was the making of me to work in those fields. A little work never hurt anybody."

"Yes, Daddy. You're right," said Aimee.

"Karen said she'd rename her school after me. It's only fair that I do something for her in return," said Blanton, watching Aimee carefully.

"My! That *was* nice of her," said Aimee, thinking, *I can't let that happen.*

And so she'd killed her stepsister, arranging it so she appeared to have vanished without a trace. She regretted it now, but what was done was done. Looking back, with Blanton having suffered a stroke and then dying not long after she killed Karen, the murder hadn't been necessary. If only she'd known!

The version she concocted was that Karen had attacked her in the swamp and she'd fought back, causing Karen to fall into the water and drown.

"You can't declare somebody dead without a body," she told Palmer and Trainor, for what felt like the thousandth time.

"But you know what happened. You were there. Why can't you go to the police? Then they can drag the swamp and find her body. I don't understand why you don't tell them. It wasn't your fault. It was self-defense. Why don't you just tell them?" In her agitation Palmer had chewed off her lipstick.

"Because the swamp is huge. It's full of alligators. An alligator may have eaten her. In fact I'm sure that's what must have happened, because otherwise the bird watchers and hikers who go back there would have reported seeing a body. Dragging the swamp wouldn't do any good. She's gone," Aimee said.

"So what are we supposed to do? Wait seven years for her to be declared dead? I am not about to wait seven years to get my *Titanic* escape room," said Palmer.

"It's four years in Georgia, not seven."

"Four years is almost as bad," Palmer replied.

"Hey! I got an idea for how we can get the money," said Trainor suddenly.

The women looked at him suspiciously. His previous schemes for raising money had usually ended in disaster.

"Aimee, you got a castle in Germany, right? Why not sell it? Then you can loan me and Palmer the money we need and you can use the rest to buy your island. Easy-peasy! Whaddya say?" Trainor looked pleased with himself for coming up with such a brilliant solution.

Aimee drank her mint julep. "Because *Schloss Wilgonhöfferen* is an albatross."

"What? I thought it was a castle," said Trainor.

"It's a metaphor. It refers to a poem where a sailor killed a big bird called an albatross and after that everything sucked," Aimee said, thinking how Trainor was a total idiot. "I can't sell *Schloss Wilgonhöfferen*; it doesn't belong to me. It didn't even belong to Franz-Albert, not really. It belongs to his family. He only got to live there because he was the oldest male heir in a direct line of descent from one of his ancestors who did a favor for Frederic the First. The king gave him a title in return, along with *Schloss Wilgonhöfferen*."

"The title makin' him a mandrake," said Trainor, nodding knowingly.

"Margrave, not mandrake," said Aimee wearily. Trainor never could get Franz-Albert's title right. "It's a prince, only it's a prince of the Holy Roman Empire, which doesn't exist anymore."

"Well, if you can't sell it, can you rent it out? Lease it to a hotel chain? People would pay big money to stay in a castle," said Palmer.

"Not this castle. It looks like the one where Doctor Frankenstein lived. The part where Franz-Albert stayed was all right, but the rest is full of moth-eaten tapestries and rusted suits of armor. Nobody in their right mind would want to stay there. Besides, one of Franz-Albert's nephews is the new margrave and he doesn't like me. He'd never give his approval so forget about it."

Jubilee came in carrying a leather-bound photo album she'd found in the library. "Mommy, look! Here's a picture of the lady in the dinosaur plant house," she said. The album was open to an eight-by-ten-inch black-and-white photo of Blanton standing beside a woman on the portico at White Oaks.

"That's her," said Jubilee, pointing to the woman in the picture.

It was Karen.

CHAPTER EIGHT –
HOW THEY MAKE SURE SOMEONE'S DEAD

The photograph must have been taken during an annual event called the Holly Jolly Holiday House Tour, judging by the garlands wrapped around the portico's Corinthian columns and the big evergreen wreath on the front door. The tour was a charity fundraiser put on in December by the Cobbs Chamber of Commerce. Blanton, as a past president of the chamber, was expected to take part by throwing open the gates to White Oaks and allowing paying members of the public the privilege of viewing some of the rooms.

An enormous balsam tree would go up in the entry hall in front of the double-reverse spiral staircase, filling the house with its tangy, woodsy scent. The tree would be strung with twinkling lights and decorated with candy canes and gingerbread men and delicate blown-glass ornaments that had been in the Trapnell family's possession for many generations.

Every year, despite red velvet ropes placed in front of the doors of rooms which weren't part of the tour, inevitably some mishap would occur. A child would break one of the Christmas tree ornaments, or the woodwork would get scratched, or wads of chewing gum would be mashed into the marble floor tiles. Occasionally someone would slip under one of the velvet ropes and be discovered snooping around in a room that was off-limits.

To Blanton, who disliked strangers strolling through his home and critiquing his possessions, the tours were nerve-wracking events. He once came upon a woman in the library, an imposing chamber with a coffered ceiling. Among its furnishings was a handsome pair of beaux-arts red oak tables with a hand-rubbed finish. They were designed by architects John Carrère and Thomas Hastings and were identical to ones in the Adam R.

Rose Reading Room of the main branch of the New York Public Library at Fifth Avenue and 42nd Street. Carrère and Thomas Hastings designed that, too.

The woman was eating a granola bar and leafing through a copy of *Treasure Island.*

"I read this when I was in school," she told Blanton happily.

He cleared his throat. "Madam, that's a first edition."

"That's nice," she said, chewing away, unperturbed.

"It's worth over twenty thousand dollars."

"That much? My goodness!"

"Stop eating! You're getting crumbs in it. You'll ruin it, you imbecilic cow! You're not supposed to be in here! Get out!" Blanton roared, tearing the book out of her hands. "Out! Out! Now!"

"You're being very rude," she told him.

"Out!" he shouted, pointing a trembling finger at the door.

Enraged, he stomped into the entry hall and ordered the startled tour-goers to leave.

"We just got here, me and my wife. We paid five dollars each. You can't kick us out," a man wearing an Atlanta Falcons cap said indignantly.

"Yes I can. Scram, all of you. Go on, get out," Blanton said, making shooing motions with his hands.

When the final tour-goer had been evicted, he slammed the front door and locked it, leaving them milling around in confusion outside, wondering whether the promised tour of the conservatories had been canceled.

It got so that Blanton's expulsion of the paying guests became an unofficial but much-loved tradition of the Holly Jolly Holiday House Tour. Citizens of Cobbs and the neighboring communities agreed that it didn't really feel like Christmas if a year went by and he didn't do it.

Aimee surmised that the photograph in the album had been taken by a photographer for the *Pontahatcha Times-Observer.* That was a weekly newspaper published in the neighboring town of Pontahatcha. Pontahatcha wasn't much, as towns went, but it was a flourishing metropolis compared to Cobbs.

The photograph had the grainy, poorly composed look typical of small-time newspaper photography. In it Blanton appeared to be about eighty. His hair was naturally jet black and would remain so to the end of his days. There was a resigned, martyred expression on his face, as if he were an elderly Sydney Carton sacrificing himself for the greater good. In this case, the greater good being the Holly Jolly Holiday House Tour, which he loathed, but put up with for the sake of the chamber of commerce.

Beside him stood his eldest child, Karen, his daughter by his first wife who had been a minor Hollywood movie actress. Karen wore a camel-hair car coat and had short, fiercely curled hair. Unfortunately for her, she had inherited her father's pugnacious jaw and prominent forehead instead of her mother's pretty features. Her legs were thick, as were her ankles and waist. She looked into the camera, seeming to stare directly at the three adults who were viewing the photograph in astonishment.

"That's your Aunt Karen," Trainor told Jubilee. "She's dead. That can't be the lady you saw."

"It is," the child insisted. "That's the lady who gave me the monster head."

"Impossible. Your Aunt Karen drowned," Aimee said. She asked Palmer, "Did she ever meet Karen?"

"I think she did, once or twice, but it would have been when she was a baby."

"Do you remember your Auntie Karen, honey?" Palmer asked.

"No, but Buppo Elephant came from her."

That was a stuffed elephant made of embroidered yellow cloth that Jubliee, for some reason, had dubbed Buppo. Palmer and Trainor suspected it was the handiwork of the hapless child laborers at Karen's school.

"The lady you saw in the dinosaur plant house was just someone who looked like your aunt. It couldn't have been Karen, just someone who looked like her," said Aimee.

"It was this lady in this picture right here," said Jubilee stubbornly.

Trainor spoke up. "Listen, how do we know for sure that Karen's dead?"

"Of course she'd dead. She had an accident in the swamp and she drowned. It was very sad," said Aimee. When they were around Jubilee, they were careful to refer to what happened to Karen as an accident. It was bad enough that the child knew one of her relatives drowned in the stagnant, algae-blanketed water, let alone that there had been violence involved.

"If she's not dead, then she's done a good job of pretending to be. According to that private detective we hired she hasn't used any of her credit cards or taken money out of any of her accounts using an ATM in six months. Nobody's seen her at any of her houses, not in Nepal, or Hawaii or Savannah. She hasn't been at her school. She's definitely dead."

"I heard of a woman who dropped out of sight for forty years," said Trainor. "She was part of one of those revolutionary student groups they used to have. Her and some other student radicals made a bomb that went off in some kind of government building, an Army recruiting office, I think it was. They looked for her for years without finding her until she gave herself up. Turns out she was livin' in a little town in Michigan all that time, workin' in a bakery with a husband and six kids, none of who knew she used to be a mad bomber."

"I doubt Karen has assumed a new life in Michigan," Aimee told him. "Things aren't like they used to be. You can't breeze into a town and go, 'Hi! I'm new here and I need a job. Can I work here?' And they hire you, no questions asked. They do background checks now, and they want your social security number. This whole conversation is ridiculous. Karen is dead. The woman Jubilee saw was somebody who looked like her."

"I still say we should have told the private investigator the whole story about how Karen drowned in the swamp. Just telling him that we were unable to contact her to tell her that her father died seems like the wrong way to go about it," said Palmer.

"Don't start that up again. We know she's dead. We told the police we don't know where she is. That's it. She'll be declared dead, eventually. No need to complicate things by changing our story. Let's concentrate on getting Judge Sparks to assign a new executor," Aimee said.

Jubilee had been studying the picture of her grandfather and Karen. She turned to her father. "What if Gong-Gong's not dead?" she asked, referring to Blanton by the name she used for him.

"He'd dead," said Trainor. "Your poor old Gong-Gong has gone home to Jesus."

"But what if he hasn't? What if you only think he's dead, the way you think Aunt Karen's dead?"

"We know your Gong-Gong's dead, honey," said Palmer.

"But how?" the child insisted. "How do you know?"

"We had to identify his body after he died in the nursing home," said Aimee irritably. In her opinion Palmer and Trainor were too lenient with

Jubilee for allowing her to keep pestering them with questions. The late Deidre Trapnell, mother of Marsh, Trainor and Aimee, wouldn't have put up with that for five seconds. She would have spanked the living daylights out of her and sent her to her room for getting on her nerves.

"But what if he was only pretending to be dead?"

"Well, then he got dead for real when Mister Chapman embalmed him," said Aimee, tired of this conversation.

"What's embalmed?" asked Jubilee.

"It's something people like Mister Chapman do to dead bodies, people who run funeral homes. I don't think it would be appropriate to go into it in any more detail than that, not until you're older," Aimee said.

Jubilee was getting worked up. She stamped her foot. "I'm not a baby. I want to know. What does Mister Chapman do to dead people? Tell me!"

Aimee got up off the sofa. "I'm exhausted. I'm going upstairs to have a bath. I'll tell Louetta I only want a bowl of soup and a salad for dinner. She can send it up to my room."

"I'll go with you," said Palmer.

As they exited the Gentlemen's Parlor they could hear Trainor explaining the embalming process to Jubilee. "Okay, first they drain out all the blood. Then they cut them open and take out the guts..."

"Eww! That's disgusting," said Jubilee, horrified. "They don't really do that, do they Daddy?"

"Yeah, they do, and there's more. Listen to this," Trainor said.

"Somebody's going to have nightmares tonight," Palmer said as she and Aimee walked down the back passage toward the kitchen.

As they passed her father's office Aimee glanced inside. As always, it came as a shock not to see him in there. "Curiosity killed the cat," she said. "Next time maybe she'll think twice before she insists on hearing about something she's too young to know."

CHAPTER NINE – BINGO SPARKS' VISITOR

The next day they dropped Jubilee off at the home of a little girl named Ainsley. Jubliee played with Ainsley when she came to Cobbs and she liked to lord it over her. Ainsley was a placid, good-natured child and didn't seem to mind.

"Ainsley, guess what? My daddy got me a pony!" Jubilee announced. "She's a purebred Connemara pony. She came with papers. Her name is Doddy Hollow Farm's Wind Blossom. She cost a lot of money. She cost more than your daddy's car!"

That was inaccurate. Ainsley's father drove a Lexus. Wind Blossom, while expensive, hadn't cost nearly as much as the Lexus.

"I've never seen a Connemara pony," said Ainsley.

"You will when you come to Atlanta. You'll see Wind Blossom and you'll see my house. It's much bigger than your house. You won't believe how big my house is compared to yours," Jubilee said.

Ainsley lived in an 11,000-square-foot house on Fortson Avenue, the best residential street in Cobbs. It had a three-car garage and six bedrooms and overlooked the golf course. To hear Jubilee talk, it might as well have been a wretched sharecropper's shack.

"It's not nice to brag," Palmer chided her. Palmer bragged frequently, but she did so in such a way that it wasn't overt but was nonetheless effective in producing pangs of envy in her friends and acquaintances.

"Trainor's taking me to St. John again," she'd say with an air of resignation, as if it were a penal colony and not what was sometimes referred to as the Beverly Hills of the Caribbean. "I wish we could go someplace else, but he bought a condominium there and he likes to keep an eye on it."

Ainsley's mother came to the door and Palmer handed Jubilee over to her. "Thanks for looking after Jubilee. We'll be back in a couple of hours. We're going to the county seat to see Judge Sparks. It has to do with my father-in-law's will. There are so many details involved in an estate of that size. We're just about plumb wore out." She puffed out her cheeks and rolled her eyes to illustrate how wore out they were.

Ainsley's mother, like all the residents of Cobbs, knew Blanton had been a very rich man. His obituary in the *Atlanta Journal-Constitution* stated that he was believed to be the wealthiest man in Georgia, if not in the entire South.

Ainsley's mother was practically eaten up with envy at the thought of how Palmer, already rich due to her marriage to Trainor, was about to become even richer. Ainsley's mother was five years younger than Palmer and now she used that fact to her advantage.

She smiled poisonously. "It's a shame you have to work so hard. You look tired. I was thinking just the other day about how pretty you are for someone your age, like those actresses that are getting on a little in years but are still attractive. But today when you drove up the first thing I thought was, goodness, doesn't Palmer look *tired!*"

They regarded each other in silence, each having scored a blow.

Palmer bent down to hug Jubilee. "Have a good time with Ainsley, sweetie. Maybe you girls can play one of her board games, an easy one; the kind with rules that Ainsley can understand."

With that she turned and walked away, a spring in her step.

Judge Sparks' chambers were in the hulking Richardson Romanesque courthouse at the county seat. The judge was nearing eighty and would have retired years ago, except for the fact that he had no hobbies and no interests outside of the law. For forty years he had enjoyed frowning down from the bench as he harangued miscreants about the error of their ways. Unfortunately he was becoming forgetful so a defendant he lectured about the folly of drinking and driving was likely to have been accused of committing some other offense – vandalism, for instance, or check fraud. They'd stand there, bewildered, unsure of what the judge was getting at.

For that reason Sparks had discretely been put out to pasture without his knowledge. He was allowed to preside over an occasional trial where the outcome would be obvious to anyone with half a brain, the defendant having been caught red-handed with several witnesses and plenty of damning evidence. The judge's clerk would steer him gently in the right direction in case he got sidetracked. It worked out well. It made Vance Sparks feel useful and it let the other judges devote their time to more difficult cases.

"I'll see if he's busy," said the judge's clerk, a recent graduate of the law school at Mercer University in Macon. She was bored out of her mind clerking for Judge Sparks, where the most interesting part of her day tended to be when she took his lunch order and walked to a nearby café to pick it up. The fact that the judge ordered the same thing for lunch every day – tuna salad on whole wheat with lettuce and tomato and a strawberry milkshake – was starting to get to her. Like prisoners and soldiers she kept count of how long it would be until her clerkship would be was up. In her case it was three months and sixteen days. She clung to that thought as she tapped on the door of the judge's chambers then stuck her head in. He was slumped in his big leather chair, his head on his chest, mouth open, snoring loudly.

"Judge Sparks," she said.

He snored on.

"JUDGE SPARKS!"

He lifted his head. "Huh? What? What's going on?" Wiping a thread of drool from his chin he frowned. "Granger, you needn't shout. I was deep in thought. I was pondering the complexities of an important case that's on the docket for tomorrow."

The clerk's name was not Granger. It was Jordan. Granger was the name of a woman who clerked for the judge when the frenzy over the impending approach of Y2K was reaching its peak. Jordan had given up on correcting him.

"Sorry, judge," she said, thinking, *there is no important case coming up tomorrow, or the next day, or the day after that, not unless you consider a shoplifting charge for stealing a home permanent kit and six pairs of clip-on sunglasses from the Quik 'N Pik an important case."*

"The Trapnells are here," she told him.

He sat up straight and passed a hand over his bald head as if to smooth down hair that was no longer there. "I suppose I can spare a few minutes. Send them in."

Trainor, Palmer and Aimee were ushered in and were invited to sit down. "Good to see y'all," said Judge Sparks. He beamed at Palmer. "Nicole, I declare you get prettier every day. How's your daddy? Does he still have that fishing camp on the Chattahoochee?"

Nicole was the name of Trainor's first wife. Palmer was wife number three.

"My name's Palmer," she said.

He looked at her with interest. "Is that so? Changed it, did you? I think Nicole is a nice name, but it seems all the young people are changing their names nowadays. It's gotten to be a fad, like hula hoops. So how *is* your daddy? Does he still have that fishing camp? You tell him Bingo Sparks was askin' for him. He'll know who you mean."

"Daddy's fine. He's still got the fishing camp. I'll tell him you said hi," said Palmer, having decided it was a losing battle to try and convince him she wasn't who he thought she was.

Trainor stepped in. "Judge, we was wonderin' if you appointed a new executor yet for Daddy's will."

The Judge removed the top from a glass candy jar on his desk. Proffering it to his guests he asked, "Care for a licorice whip?"

They each took one, not wanting them, but knowing he'd insist.

"I got good news for y'all," the judge said, twirling a licorice whip between his fingers.

"You appointed a new executor? We can get the will probated?" Aimee practically fell out of her chair in excitement.

The judge chuckled indulgently. "There's no need for that. It all worked out. Karen turned up. She's handling it, just like your Daddy wanted."

The Trapnells looked at one another, stunned.

Aimee spoke up. "You say Karen turned up? You saw her?"

The judge bit into his licorice whip. The gummy candy made his dentures stick together. In his struggle to free them he utilized a bent paperclip. He held up a hand as he poked and pried, as if to say *hang on a minute.* Once unstuck, it didn't stop him from taking another bite. The Trapnells waited, not believing what they'd heard, while he chewed and swallowed.

"She sat right where you're sitting now," he told Aimee. "Said she'd been away, having been detained on business, but she was back and was ready to take up her duties as executor. She apologized if her absence caused any inconvenience."

"When was this?" Trainor asked.

The judge cast his eyes to the ceiling, thinking. "I'm not sure. I got a busy calendar. It keeps me hopping. Let me ask Granger; she'll know." He buzzed his clerk. "Granger, when was Karen Trapnell here?"

They could hear Jordan sigh heavily before she responded. "Yesterday, Judge."

"Thank you, Granger," he said, turning off his intercom.

Aimee couldn't believe it. "You saw my stepsister Karen? She was here yesterday? You're sure it was her?"

The judge finished his licorice whip and fished in the jar for another. "It was her. She brought your daddy's will. Care for another licorice whip?"

CHAPTER TEN – THE COWBOY

In the opposite wing at White Oaks from the one where the Gentlemen's Parlor was located was its mirror image: the Ladies' Parlor. It had escaped Blanton's redecorating purge in the nineteen-fifties, which turned out to be a stroke of luck because the walls still bore their original hand-painted wallpaper panels. These were now worth considerably more than they were when a merchant ship's captain brought them back from China prior to the Civil War.

The wallpaper was like a window into another world, one where birds of paradise strutted in front of buildings with upturned roofs. Ladies in kimonos walked over hump-backed bridges accompanied by gentlemen in kimonos who carried tiny cages with songbirds in them.

When Aimee was a child she had loved the Ladies' Parlor best of all the rooms in the house. She liked to curl up on the plush velvet settee with the carved rosewood frame and tell herself stories about the people in the wallpaper.

She still loved the Ladies' Parlor, but now she was in no mood to admire the wallpaper. The first thing they'd done when they returned from picking up Jubilee was to dash into Blanton's office. Aimee fell to her knees in front of the big iron floor safe. She spun the combination and flung the door open.

The will, in its long white envelope, was gone.

Aimee frantically dug through the contents of the safe, finding contracts, stock certificates, deeds, old letters, bank statements, but no will.

She sat back on her heels. "Shit! Shit! Shit!"

"It's not in there?" asked Trainor.

"No."

"Are you sure?"

"Look for yourself. Shit! I can't believe it."

Trainor sorted through the documents Aimee had tossed on the floor. He held up a long white envelope and waved it triumphantly. "Look what I found!"

"The will? Boo Bear! Thank heaven!" said Palmer.

Trainor removed something from the envelope. "Nope. It's the pink slip to a car I used to have, an IROC-Z. I totaled it when me and Peach Walker were on spring break one time, down in Florida." He smiled reminiscently. "Man, I loved that car. Peach said I was too drunk to drive. I told him I wasn't, but I guess I was because I rolled it on Highway 41. Peach and me managed to crawl out just before it caught fire and exploded. Damn! How about that? Wait until I tell Peach. The pink slip to my Z. This brings back memories!"

"That's great, Trainor. I'm happy for you," Aimee said tartly. "But the problem remains: Daddy's will is gone and a strange woman is going around pretending to be Karen."

"Maybe it really is Karen," said Palmer.

"Don't start. Judge Sparks is dotty. He wouldn't know Karen from Kim Kardashian. Hell, he wouldn't know her from the woman who works at the security booth at the courthouse. Somebody got in here and took the will and now somebody pretending to be Karen is trying to steal our money."

"Steal our money? How?" asked Trainor, aghast.

"By giving the judge a counterfeit will, of course. They probably destroyed the real one. Shit!"

"How would they know the combination to the safe?" asked Palmer.

Aimee shook her head disgustedly. "They wouldn't have to. Daddy always acted like nobody could steal it because it weighs five hundred pounds, but there's no need to steal the whole safe, not if you can open it. Safes as old as this one aren't exactly high tech. A child could open it. I used to do it all the time when I was little, just for fun, to see what he had in it. I read how to do it in a magazine. All you need is a flat-head screwdriver and some patience."

She gathered the scattered documents and put them back into the safe, shutting the heavy iron door and spinning the lock. "This is what you call closing the barn door after the horse has bolted."

They trudged to the Ladies' Parlor and sat down, trying to think what to do next. Call Judge Sparks? Call the governor? Contact the private investigator they hired when they'd reported Karen missing and tell him there was an impostor at work?

Trainor stood up and stretched. "I could use somethin' to eat," he said. "My brain works better when I've had somethin' to eat. You think Louetta finished makin' that hummingbird cake?"

Their cook, Louetta Waites, was rightfully proud of her hummingbird cakes. The recipe was a closely guarded secret. Louetta's cakes were much in demand at social functions in Cobbs and the neighboring communities. She had a nice sideline going, making cakes for church suppers, birthday parties and the like. Jubilee was currently assisting her in making one, having been sworn to secrecy about what went into it.

The kitchen smelled wonderfully of freshly baked cake. The three layers were on wire cooling racks on a marble-topped table, next to a mixing bowl full of frosting, but Louetta wasn't attending to it. She and Jubilee were looking out of the window at something outside. Jubilee stood on tiptoes on a step-stool to be able to see better. Janelle and Anea, two of the maids, were there too. They stood back from the window, as if they were afraid to look outside.

"Is he still out there?" Janelle asked Louetta.

"He is. He peekin' around the opening in the hedge," she replied.

A thick, green hedge of Leland cypress surrounded three sides of a stone-paved patio where the summer kitchen used to be. The fourth side of the patio was taken up by part of the back wall of the house where the current kitchen was. When the summer kitchen was torn down a little tin box was discovered behind a loose brick in the chimney. Inside was a sinister object made of human teeth. Chicken bones were wrapped around them in the form of a cross. Blanton kept the box and its macabre contents in his office, taking it out occasionally to show visitors.

"Voodoo," he'd say, his voice tinged with awe. "They used to do Voodoo, right here in this house."

"Ohhh, peekin'! He must be crazy. Normal people don't peek," said Janelle.

"What are you doing?" asked Palmer.

Louetta whirled around, her hand on her heart. "Oh lord! You gave me a jump. There's a crazy man outside, peekin' and grinnin' like a fool."

"There he goes again," said Jubilee. "Look at him slide. How is he doing that?" She sounded intrigued.

"He slidin' again? That ain't right," said Janelle, who had opined that normal people don't peek. "Come on, Anea, let's get out of here."

"I ain't goin' outside, not when *he* out there," said Anea.

"You right; he might get us," said Janelle. "Mister Trainor, you go see what he wants."

Trainor took a step backward. "Why me?"

"You a man," she said, as if that were sufficient explanation.

She and Anea left the kitchen, casting frightened glances over their shoulders toward the window.

Trainor looked around, hoping to see the butler so he could get him to go see what the man was up to. "Where's Lee?"

"In town, doin' errands," said Louetta.

Trainor cautiously looked out the window. He could see a jug-eared middle-aged white man standing at the opening in the hedge. The man looked like a cowboy from old-time Western movies. He wore a ten-gallon hat, a chambray work shirt, blue jeans and cowboy boots. Strapped to his lean hips was a pair of six-shooters. The cowboy was doing the seemingly impossible. He glided effortlessly back and forth across the opening, like a target in a carnival shooting gallery. He grinned broadly, as if he was having a whooping good time.

"He's armed; I'm not goin' out there. I'm callin' the sheriff," Trainor said.

By the time the sheriff arrived the man, whoever he was, was gone.

Sheriff Ewell Haskins had fairly flown out to White Oaks, siren wailing, blue emergency lights flashing, accelerator pedal pressed to the floorboard of the Ford Taurus Police Interceptor that was his pride and joy. Haskins was still new enough to his position that it surprised and delighted him each time he saw the vehicle with SHERIFF emblazoned on the sides parked in his driveway.

In his haste to come to the aid of the Trapnells he had neglected to wipe his mouth before leaving a dining establishment called the Sho' Nuff Good Family Barbeque. A clownish ring of orange barbecue sauce encircled his lips when Aimee opened the front door.

Haskins pitched his voice low, trying to sound like a powerful emissary of law and order. He adjusted his leather duty belt, heavy with the various accouterments of his profession, including handcuffs, flashlight, radio, and his Smith & Wesson .38.

"Afternoon, Miz Trapnell, er, Missus von Helgern," he said. "I got here quick as I could. What's the trouble?"

"Were you having lunch?" Aimee asked.

"I had a quick bite."

"Was it barbecue?"

"Gosh! How'd you know?"

Aimee tapped her upper lip with a manicured fingernail. "Sauce."

"Aw, heck." He wiped his mouth with the back of his hand. "You probably think I'm a big slob." Haskins had hoped to impress the Trapnells with his quick response to their call for help. Now he'd screwed it up by having food on his face.

"Not at all," she said, although she did.

Haskins searched the grounds and found no sign of the intruder. His search took him as far as the entrance to the swamp. If the man had gone in there, it would require bloodhounds to track him down. Haskins considered calling the state police and asking for some to be sent out before rejecting the idea. He was intimidated by the state police, whom he correctly believed thought of him as a laughable rube along the lines of Barney Fife from *The Andy Griffith Show*. No doubt they'd refuse his request, since no crime had been committed, other than trespassing.

He examined the ground for footprints, but didn't find any except for his own. There were tire tracks in the dirt of the parking area intended for visitors to the nature preserve. Haskins photographed them, feeling like he had to do *something*. Then he went back to the house.

"He's gone," he told the Trapnells and Louetta Waites. "I'll circulate the description you gave me, but the thing is..." He paused, trying to think of how to put it. "The thing is, he didn't do anything wrong."

"He was slidin'. Slidin' an' peepin' an' grinnin'. It like to give me a heart attack," said Louetta. She dipped a spatula in the icing and began to frost the cake.

"I can see how that would be disturbing, but you say he was fully clothed? He didn't waggle his willy at you or nothing?"

"Lord, no! But the slidin' was bad enough. People don't slide like that. It's not natural," she said.

Haskins had examined the opening in the hedge where the mystery man was reported to have been sliding back and forth. He'd found no wire or rail or anything that would have permitted him to move the way the frightened witnesses described.

"His feet were touching the ground, you say? He wasn't riding a skateboard?"

The Trapnells and Louetta shook their heads.

"There wasn't, I dunno, a zip line or something back there?" Haskins asked.

"It looked like his feet were touching the ground. It was just so weird, the way he was moving," said Palmer.

"I wish we had a zip line," said Jubilee.

Haskins bent down so he was eye level with her. "Maybe your daddy will put one up for you if you're a good girl." He straightened up and winked at Trainor.

"That's a good idea. We got plenty of room outside. It'd be fun," said Trainor eagerly.

Aimee couldn't believe they were discussing installing a zip line instead of taking steps to catch the trespasser. "What do you intend to do about this, Sheriff?"

"I could come out on my day off and help put it up."

"Not the zip line, the man who was here. What are you going to do about him?"

Very little, it turned out, aside from passing on the man's description to the deputies and telling them to keep an eye out. "Maybe you could put up no-trespassing signs and get a couple of big dogs," Haskins suggested. Seamus had come into the kitchen and was getting underfoot, excited by their agitated voices. Haskins patted him on the head.

"This here's a good old dog, but what you want is some mean dogs, like pit bulls."

"Daddy told me his daddy had a pair of mastiffs once. They was called Biter and Fighter. He said they was the meanest dogs he ever saw. We could get some dogs like that," said Trainor.

"Don't expect me to take care of them," said Louetta. "I got enough to do."

CHAPTER ELEVEN – AIMEE FAILS TO TAKE A HINT

The cowboy appeared again the following day. He was with a group of birdwatchers who were going into the swamp. Unlike the previous day when he'd been gliding as if he were on rails, he walked normally, ambling along behind the others.

He had on the ten-gallon hat and the clothes he'd worn previously. Aimee watched him from the garden where she was cutting flowers. Although she was quite a distance away, he must have sensed her eyes on him because he turned and placed two fingers against the brim of his hat in an ironic salute. Like the previous day his face wore that unnerving Cheshire Cat grin. Aimee called the sheriff, but when Haskins got there, the man was gone.

She spotted him again later that day, walking down the road that ran past White Oaks. Once again he saluted her and once again he was gone by the time the sheriff arrived. If he hadn't been wearing a pair of six-shooters Aimee would have approached him and demanded to know what he wanted. Aimee wasn't foolhardy. Maybe the guns were toys, but maybe they were real. She wasn't about to take a chance on finding out.

"It's a public road. If he was walkin' down your driveway, I'd arrest him in no time flat," Haskins told her. "No time at all, just boom! You're under arrest." He hoped he sounded convincing. He had never arrested anyone for walking down a driveway before. He wasn't sure if it would be legal for him to do so. "If he's not threatening you in any way, I don't see what we can do about it, even if we do catch him, which we definitely will," he added after Aimee gave him a cold look.

"We'll catch him, don't you worry none." He wondered what infraction the man could be accused of committing. The nature preserve belonged to the state of Georgia. The grounds of White Oaks were private property, but they weren't posted against trespassing. The man could claim he didn't know he shouldn't have been there and get let off with a warning.

"It's always an honor to come out here and talk to you, Miz Aimee," Haskins told her, twisting his broad-brimmed uniform hat in his hands. "Both a duty and an honor."

"Uh-huh," she said.

He took a deep breath and decided to go for it. "Just the other day my wife was sayin' how nice it would be, now that I'm sheriff, if we could join the country club."

"What's stopping you?"

"Well, nothin', really, except I gotta get nominated by somebody who's a member." He waited, eyebrows raised expectantly, hoping she'd volunteer.

"You shouldn't have any trouble with that, I imagine," said Aimee. "I have things to do. Lee will show you out."

Haskins left, feeling dejected. He knew his wife would demand to know as soon as he got home if he'd approached Aimee about nominating him for country club membership. What was he going to tell her? That he'd hinted and Aimee hadn't taken the hint? His wife would tell him to quit hinting and come right out and ask, but he was afraid the answer would be no. Aimee wanted him to apprehend the trespasser and he'd failed to do so, making it unlikely that she'd be in the mood to grant him any favors. He could always ask someone else to nominate him, but Blanton Trapnell had founded the country club. The club's flag and insignia on its letterhead were black and red, the colors of Blanton's beloved University of Georgia. To have his name put forward for membership by one of the Trapnell children would carry considerable weight. It would practically guarantee admission.

Haskins became determined to catch the trespasser. He began cruising the roads around White Oaks, hoping to encounter him. If he did, he would charge him with committing some offense and haul him in, even if he had to make something up. Pleasing Aimee by capturing the mysterious cowboy was vitally important for his family's future. Once he was admitted to the country club, the sky would be the limit, in terms of social and political advancement, or so he thought. The cachet he credited to membership in

Cobbs' dinky little country club was touching, like a child's belief in Santa Claus.

Haskins pictured himself remarking casually to the state attorney general, "When I was playing golf at the club down in Cobbs the other day..." and having that worthy gentleman view him with new respect. It didn't matter that Haskins didn't know how to play golf. He could learn; all he needed was a membership card in his wallet and the sticker with the club's red and black crest on the windshield of his personal vehicle. Then he was certain he would be admitted into the ranks of the elite.

Trainor and Palmer had gone back to Atlanta with Jubilee, explaining to Aimee that the child needed to go to school. None of the servants at White Oaks lived in, leaving Aimee alone in the house at night. She usually didn't mind being alone, but the enormous house felt spooky without Blanton's noisy, cantankerous presence to enliven it. There were too many rooms standing hushed and empty. Small noises that went unnoticed in the daytime – old floorboards creaking as they expanded and contracted, cool air whispering through the air-conditioning vents, the *womp* of the refrigerator's motor turning on and off – were magnified at night. After the servants left for the day Aimee found herself keeping to her room, bringing Seamus in there with her for company.

She went back to see Judge Sparks, trying to convince him that the woman who had claimed to be Karen was an imposter. He didn't seem impressed when she told him that none of the family had seen Karen in months. He was similarly unimpressed when she told him the private investigator they'd hired to find her came up empty, concluding that it appeared Karen had vanished off the face of the earth.

"He must not have been good at finding people," the judge said. He leaned back in his big leather chair and laced his fingers behind his head. "When I was starting out practicing law, the firm I worked for had a private investigator they used named Jessop Abernathy. Old Jessop was a real character. He always wore a slouch hat and carried a pocket watch, which was unusual, even back then. He used to be on the Atlanta police force, so he knew how to get things done, even if it meant bending the law a little. I remember one time..."

Sparks launched into a lengthy, convoluted tale about a payroll theft at a soft-drink bottling company. There was a woman involved, a *femme fatale* whom he described as "a real hotsy-totsy." Aimee listened politely, fuming inside.

"Abernathy sounds like quite a guy," she said when he was done. "Getting back to the investigator we hired, he came highly recommended. He told us he had a success rate of ninety-five percent. If he couldn't find Karen I think it means she's dead. The woman who came to see you wasn't her."

Sparks regarded her brightly, his head tilted to one side, like a parrot.

"It was your stepsister. I'd know her anywhere. I don't know why the fellow you hired couldn't locate her. Remember, a success rate of ninety-five percent means he failed five percent of the time."

Aimee couldn't argue with that. She knew Karen was dead, but she couldn't tell Sparks that.

"Can I at least see the will she gave you?"

"No can do, young lady. I passed it on to the clerk of the probate court.

"What did it say?"

Sparks looked shocked. "I can't reveal that."

"Why not?"

"Nobody but the grantor – that's the person who makes a will – and the executor are entitled to know what's in it. From what you told me, your daddy informed you that his estate was to be divided equally between you and your brothers and stepsister." He smiled fondly at her, as if he found her anxiety adorable. "There's no need to fret. It'll all work out in due course. After probate's been completed the beneficiaries will be notified. Care for a licorice whip?"

Aimee's phone calls to Marsh went directly to voice mail. He must be somewhere overseas, selling weapons. Maybe he'd been kidnapped by terrorists, either ones he sold weapons to or enemies of ones he sold weapons to. Possibly he was dead. Aimee wouldn't be a bit surprised if he was, considering the kind of life he led.

Marsh was the most complex of the Trapnell siblings. Trainor was as uncomplicated as a paramecium. Aimee cared for no one except for herself and her son Benjamin, whom she loved fiercely. She would give her life for Benjamin without hesitation. In addition, Aimee loved being admired, and she loved her snakes. She loved designing clothes, and she loved being rich. Those were the extent of her interests.

Marsh, however, was more complex. Yes, he sold weapons to despots and dictators, but he also sold them to freedom fighters and members of resistance movements. He was an equal-opportunity arms dealer, believing everyone should be entitled to his wares on an even basis. He also gave lavishly (and anonymously) to charity. He had a moral code, albeit an odd one. He didn't really understand it himself, other than the vague idea that his disparate activities were somehow balancing things out.

It was annoying that he couldn't be reached. Aimee didn't especially like Marsh, but she respected him. If anyone could survive a nuclear war or an invasion by space aliens he could. He had, after all, saved the world from destruction during that horrible affair of the sigul of Jörmungandr. If anyone could figure out what was going on, it would be he.

Aimee and Trainor and Palmer's only consolation was that they had copies of Blanton's will. They could challenge the results of the will which the woman pretending to be Karen had submitted, but it would take time and would eat up a lot of money in legal fees. It was maddening. Who was this woman, and what was she trying to achieve?

Aimee soon found out.

CHAPTER TWELVE – THE NIGHT VISITOR

Aimee was in bed in her room at White Oaks. It was late at night and she was listening to music, hoping it would help her relax. Seamus had been sleeping in his basket when suddenly he stood up. He went to the door and scratched at it.

"You want to go out? Okay, let me get dressed," Aimee told him.

The dog scratched at the door again and whined.

"Give me a second," Aimee told him. She pulled on shorts and a t-shirt and slipped her feet into loafers. "You went outside two hours ago. This had better not be a false alarm."

She opened the door. Seamus bolted out of the room and down the broad second-floor hallway leading to the double-reverse staircase. He raced down the stairs. Aimee leaned over the railing of the gallery. "Slow down!" she called, but he was already at the bottom.

The antique Baccarat crystal chandelier hanging from the ceiling of the entry hall was lit, as it always was at night, the dimmer switch turned down to its lowest setting. Aimee saw the dog dash past the Gentlemen's Parlor, heading in the direction of the library and Blanton's office.

"You must really have to go outside," Aimee muttered, hurrying down the stairs.

Halfway across the shadowy entry hall she stopped. There was a light on inside the library. It cast a buttery golden glow against the cypress floorboards of the passage leading to the rooms at the rear of the house. Aimee had been in the library earlier, but she was sure she'd turned off all the lights before going upstairs. Or had she? Maybe she'd forgotten and left one on.

Her mind flashed to the cowboy. Could he have gotten inside? It was possible. The house had no security system. Blanton had been violently opposed to the idea. There were at least a half-dozen doors leading to the outside. The front door and the kitchen door were always locked at night, but as for the others? Aimee mentally cataloged them: the delivery entrance; the set of tall double doors leading into the house from the *porte-cochère*; the French doors in the breakfast room; the door in the sunroom, and the Dutch door in the room where they kept things like boots and tennis rackets and Seamus' leash. She wasn't sure if Lee had locked all of them before leaving for the day to go to his apartment in Cobbs. He was supposed to, but he may have forgotten one.

White Oaks had been added onto in stages. The original framed blueprints were hanging in the library. They dated to 1831. The house had grown considerably since then. As far as Aimee knew there were no plans showing it in its current form. There could be a door no one knew about.

No one, that is, except for whoever might be in the library.

Just then a low voice came from the library. "Good boy, Seamus," it said.

Aimee froze.

Cautiously she poked her head in the room. At the far end wing chairs were grouped around a fireplace with a carved black marble surround. Someone was seated in one of them. The chair's high back was to her. All Aimee could see was an arm in a white shirt sleeve reaching out a hand to stroke Seamus' head.

"Good boy," the voice repeated.

Seamus was panting happily, his tongue hanging out. He looked at Aimee as if to say, *See who's come to visit us!*

Her loafers whispered on the thick pile of the gold and indigo antique Bakhtiari Persian rug as Aimee slowly walked down the long room, past bookshelves rising to the coffered ceiling. As she reached the fireplace, she turned to face the chair's occupant.

It was Karen.

She'd lost a lot of weight and there were purplish shadows under her eyes. In her lap was an object which was horribly familiar to Aimee: a flowered chintz beanbag filled with ball bearings, shaped like a frog.

"Hi, Aimee. I see you remember Petulia Puddlehopper," said Karen.

"Where did..." Aimee's words came out as a cracked whisper. She cleared her throat. "Where did you find it?"

"Upstairs on the third floor, in the room next to the old nursery. There were some toys in there. I guess they belong to Jubilee. I saw her in one of the conservatories and gave her a present."

"The monster head."

Karen laughed. "Is that what you call it? It's not a monster. It's Mahākāla. He's a guardian and a protector. I picked it up on my travels and thought Jubilee might like it. Tell me, why would something you used to bludgeon me be mixed in with Jubilee's toys?"

"I gave it to her," said Aimee.

Karen laughed again, sounding genuinely tickled. "You whacked me over the head with it, thinking you killed me, and then you gave it to your seven-year-old niece. Aimee, you are something else."

"I'm sorry I tried to kill you," said Aimee.

Karen studied her, unsmiling. "I believe you are. Alert the media! Aimee Louise Trapnell Monteleone von Helgern actually has a conscience. Will wonders ever cease?"

"How long have you been here?" Aimee asked.

"In this house? About a week. This place is so big thirty people could be hiding in here and nobody would notice. I went down to the kitchen at night after the staff went home and you were tucked up in your bed, dreaming about whatever someone like you dreams about. I got something to eat and drink. Had a look around. Went into Daddy's office..."

Aimee sank into a wing chair. Seamus went over and rubbed his face against her knee, looking up at her, concern in his amber eyes.

"You're the one who took Daddy's will out of the safe," she said.

"That's right."

Aimee's eyes widened as she realized something. "You must have been the one who ate the cornbread and the collard greens! Louetta was furious. She blamed the maids. She blamed *me*!"

"Relax, I'll confess to Louetta. Aren't you interested in what I did with Daddy's will?"

"You threw it away, or you burned it. Then you went to Judge Sparks – it really was you – and you gave him a will naming you as sole beneficiary. You must have forged Daddy's signature. God knows it was easy to reproduce his scrawl. You forged the signatures of the witnesses, too: Hillman and Bestie. Hillman's in federal custody and Bestie's got Alzheimer's, so it would be hard to prove those aren't their signatures. Good job, Karen, but you're not going to win this. Trainor and Marsh and I will take you to court, but good job anyway. This will cost a fortune in legal fees."

Karen looked sad. "Do you really think I would do that?"

"Well, didn't you?"

"No."

Karen crossed her legs and straightened the crease in her white linen trousers. She'd apparently made use of the iron and ironing board in the laundry room while she was roaming around the house at night. "You're wrong. I took the will – Daddy's real will – to Judge Sparks. I told him I'd been away on business and that's why I didn't do it sooner. I didn't say a word about you knocking me into the water and leaving me for dead. I will never say anything about that. Not to Vance Sparks, not to anyone. You have my word on that."

She stared at Aimee, her chin defiantly outthrust. There was a ghostly echo of Blanton in her expression.

"Really?" asked Aimee.

"Really," said Karen. "All is forgiven. Cross my heart and hope to die. Again. Not that I was dead before, but you know what I mean; I'm sincere. Not a word will I say to anyone."

Her voice thickened. "Listen, Aimee. I had it coming. I tried to kill you that time I pushed you down the stairs and broke your arm. You were ten. I was almost thirty. I should have known better. I *did* know better, but I was mad that Daddy made a fuss over you while practically ignoring me. Then I poured a pot of boiling water on your feet." Her voice rose in anguish. "What kind of a monster pours boiling water on a child?"

"The same kind of monster who bludgeons blood kin and knocks them into a swamp," said Aimee.

Karen took a tissue from the box on the table at her elbow. She blew her nose and laughed ruefully. "You're right. The Trapnells have always been monsters. You and I are par for the course."

"Where were you all this time? How did you survive? You fell in the water and didn't come up. I waited a long time," Aimee said. She'd stood there, her heart pounding, clutching Petulia Puddlehopper and waiting to see if Karen would surface, sputtering mad, clumps of green algae streaming from her hair. If she had, Aimee had intended to hit her again.

"I'll tell you, but it's a long story and I'm thirsty. Let's go in the kitchen," said Karen.

CHAPTER THIRTEEN – THE NEST

Aimee flicked on a row of light switches on the kitchen wall, illuminating the big room. The overhead florescent lights buzzed faintly behind their frosted glass panels. The countertops and floor gleamed, spotless as an operating room. The kitchen smelled of bleach and the lemon-scented dishwashing liquid Louetta used.

Karen went to the refrigerator and got a bottle of water. Then she went into the walk-in freezer and brought out a gallon of chocolate ice cream. She set it on the marble-topped kitchen table.

"Want some?" she asked Aimee.

"Okay," Aimee replied. She still found it hard to believe that Karen had forgiven her. She moved closer to the knives in the knife block, just in case.

"I'm not going to stab you," said Karen, her back to Aimee.

"How did you know what I was thinking?"

Karen turned around. She held two glass bowls and two spoons. "Because I know how your mind works. You've got a wild imagination; you always did. You were thinking I was biding my time, waiting for you to let your guard down and then I'd get my revenge by stabbing you to death with one of those butcher knives over there. Want some ice cream? I didn't poison it."

"That's reassuring. Thanks, I'll have some." Aimee pulled up a chair. "Are you allowed to eat ice cream? You're still a Buddhist, right?"

Karen sat down. "I'm still a Buddhist. We're allowed to have ice cream if we want to." She scooped ice cream into a dish and pushed it across the table to Aimee. "Actually, I'm a nun."

Aimee paused, her spoon halfway to her mouth. "A Catholic nun? How can you be both a Buddhist and a Catholic nun?"

"I'm a Buddhist nun."

"Since when?"

"Since a couple of years ago. I became acquainted with the abbess at the monastery near where my school was. She's an amazing woman. She helped me take the vows to become a novitiate. It transformed my life. It would take a long time to explain it all to you, but I'll answer the two questions people usually ask me when they find out I'm a Buddhist nun: am I celibate? Yes, I am. Why is my head shaved? It's a symbol of my having renounced worldly attachments."

"But your head's not shaved."

Karen removed her wig, revealing a gleaming bald scalp. "Ta-da! I'm in mufti. I got this wig so Judge Sparks would recognize me when I brought him Daddy's will. If I need to be out in public down here, I thought I should blend in with the locals. They probably consider Unitarians to be a bizarre cult. They wouldn't know what to make of a Buddhist nun with a shaved head."

"You don't look too bad like that," said Aimee. She pursed her lips and considered her stepsister. "I wonder how I'd look with my head shaved?"

"It's not intended to be a fashion statement, Aimee." Karen put the wig back on.

"You said where your school was. Isn't it still there?"

"It is, but I no longer own it. I signed it over to my assistant, Kaamya Gurung. She's running it now, under the supervision of a board of directors. The students are learning a STEM curriculum."

In response to Aimee's blank look she said, "That stands for science, technology, engineering and mathematics. The girls still make handicrafts, but only for art class, not for sale. I ended the connection with Himalayan Village Treasures. There are plenty of other places they can buy from, but they'll no longer be buying anything made at the Dhaulagiri School for Girls. Before I left, I bought the school forty new PCs, the best money could buy. I also had the dorms renovated. As a final parting gift I gave them an endowment from my trust fund. The Nepali government makes an annual donation and various charities from throughout the world help keep the school up and running. I made sure all of the charities were on the level and weren't a front for money laundering or human trafficking or any other criminal activity."

Aimee was stunned. This was unlike the Karen she used to know. "Did you take a vow of poverty or something?"

"Yes."

"Daddy was right; he said you were like Mother Teresa."

Karen snorted. "Hardly."

Aimee felt a rising excitement. If Karen took a vow of poverty, then maybe she wouldn't want her one-quarter share of Blanton's estate.

"Forget it," said Karen.

"What?"

"I'm not going to give you my share of Daddy's estate. I'm donating it to charity."

Aimee's mouth fell open. "Are you psychic?"

"No. I don't have any special powers, not really, although something happened, something I need help with. I'll get to that in a minute."

Karen scooped ice cream into her bowl. "As I said, I know how you think. You were hoping I'd give you my share of the inheritance because I felt bad about pushing you down the stairs."

"Tell me how you survived after you fell into the swamp." Aimee met Karen's cool gray gaze and amended the question. "Tell me how you survived after I hit you and made you fall into the swamp. I was sure you drowned."

Karen took a drink of bottled water. "I was jet-lagged from the long flight. When you told me we were going to surprise Daddy by my showing up unannounced I didn't suspect anything. You met me in Miami and brought me back here, saying we'd go in the house, but first you wanted me to see some rare birds that were nesting in the nature preserve. What kind were they?"

"Tricolored herons," said Aimee.

Karen nodded. "Right. I forgot what you said they were called. I was happy that you were being so friendly, picking me up at the Waffle House by the airport and inviting me to go for a walk with you. I thought it meant things were going to be better between us." She gave a short laugh. "Boy was I wrong! You showed me Petulia Puddlehopper, saying it was your mascot."

Karen had brought the beanbag frog into the kitchen with her. It sat slumped on the table, its red-lipped mouth grinning foolishly. Aimee tried to avoid looking at it, but her gaze kept returning to it. She thought, *I wonder what she wants? Is she going to get even with me? She said she wasn't, but what if she was lying?*

Karen went on, "It was dark, but there was almost a full moon. You had a penlight with you and you used it to light our way. We walked pretty far into the nature preserve. You kept saying it was only a little bit farther. Then you pointed to where you said the heron's nest was. I turned to look and out of the corner of my eye I saw you swing your arm. You smacked me in the head with this." She shook Petulia Puddlehopper, as if for emphasis.

"I literally saw stars. I fell in the water. I was scared to come up in case you hit me again so I crawled along the muddy bottom, holding my breath. Something brushed against my leg. I thought it was an alligator. That scared me even more. Maybe it was a fish, or maybe it was a clump of water weeds. I bumped my head against one of the pilings of the dock, making my head hurt even more. I scooted underneath the dock. There's space under there that's above the water line, not much, but enough for me to float on my back and poke my lips up to get a little bit of air. I stayed down there, taking sips of air, for a long time. It could have been an hour; I had no way of telling. My head was pounding. I threw up. Finally I couldn't stand it any longer. I was weak from shock and loss of blood. I knew I had to get out of there before I passed out. I squeezed out from under the dock and looked around to see if you were still there. I thought you might be hiding and would jump out at me."

"I'm sorry," Aimee said. She'd thought it would be simple: one blow over the head and Karen would be gone forever, clean and easy.

"There's more," said Karen. "My head throbbed until I thought it was going to burst wide open like a rotten tomato. Blood ran down my face, getting in my eyes and making my vision blurry. It was dark as the inside of a cow, as Daddy used to say. The vegetation back there is thick and there's kudzu and Spanish moss hanging from the trees. It was hard to see where I was going. I stumbled around trying to find the way out, making false starts and doubling back. Twice I tripped and fell full-length into the mud. I kept hearing noises. It was probably just animals and birds, but I thought it was you, following me. I walked faster and almost fell over a mound of sticks and mud and grass. I thought at first it was a beaver dam, but it was an alligator's nest."

"Was there an alligator in it?" asked Aimee.

"There was. Mama gator stuck her head out and hissed. I backed away and beat a hasty retreat. Alligators are fast and she could have caught me if she wanted to, but she stayed with her eggs. Eventually I found my way out to the parking lot by the entrance to the nature preserve."

"I'm sorry you went through all that," Aimee said again. "Why didn't you come to the house?"

"And take a chance that you'd try and kill me again? No. I was lucky. There was a car in the parking lot. Two teenagers were in it, doing what teenagers do when they're parked in a secluded spot at night. I knocked on the window, and they screamed. I was covered with mud and must have looked like the Creature from the Black Lagoon. Once they realized I wasn't going to harm them they were friendly. I told them I'd been hiking and had fallen into the water, losing my backpack with my wallet and phone and change of clothes in it.

"They drove me to the girl's house in Pontahatcha. She let me take a shower. Her mother gave me some clothes she was going to donate to charity. Then they drove me to the bus station. I called a friend who paid for a bus ticket. Two hours later I was on a bus bound for Mississippi."

Karen finished her water. She rinsed the ice cream bowls and spoons in the sink before putting them in the dishwasher. Then she sat back down at the table.

"Where were you? You were missing for six months," said Aimee.

"I was in a Buddhist monastery."

"You went back to Nepal?"

"A Buddhist monastery in Mississippi."

"There are Buddhist monasteries in Mississippi? I didn't know that."

"There are Buddhist monasteries all over," said Karen. "I knew someone who lives there. He paid for my bus ticket. The monastery has an infirmary where they treated me for a concussion and a nasty intestinal bug I got from swallowing swamp water. I stayed there, helping out, praying and meditating, trying to get my head straight. That's where I got the idea to try something."

For the first time since she began telling her story Karen hesitated. "You're not going to like this," she said.

"What? What's going on?" Aimee asked nervously. She'd thought she was alone in the house until Karen appeared. Karen had said dozens of people could be hiding inside. Had she brought someone with her? She looked toward the back stairs. Had she heard a board creak? Was someone up there, listening?

"I made something and it got out of control," Karen said. "I'm afraid it's turned evil."

"What? What did you make?" asked Aimee.

"It looks like a cowboy, but it's not."

CHAPTER FOURTEEN –
AN IMAGINARY FRIEND YOU CAN SEE

"This is how it all began," said Karen. "One of the books in the monastery's library was a biography of a scholar and explorer named Alexandra David-Néel. I became fascinated by her. She was born in 1868 and lived to be one hundred and one years old. From the very beginning she was unusual.

"When she was fifteen, she ran away from home. She traveled all over Europe, on foot and on a bicycle. Girls weren't supposed to do that back in those days. When she was twenty-one she went to India, where she studied Sanskrit. Later she became an opera singer, performing with the Opera Company of Hanoi."

"They should make a movie about her," said Aimee. "Movies about strong women who do things are popular now."

Karen looked at her, surprised. "That actually might be a good idea. David-Néel had a remarkable life. She met a lot of important people, including His Holiness, the thirteenth Dalai Lama. She was the first Western woman to be granted an audience with him. She became interested in Buddhism while she was living in Paris. She later became a disciple of the Gomchen of Lachen. He was the abbot of the Phodong monastery in a mountain village in Sikkim in northeast India, near the Tibetan border. She spent two years at Phodong, studying and meditating, writing and translating texts in the monastery's library. She was fifty-five in 1924, when she decided to become the first Western woman to enter Lhasa."

"Where's that?" asked Aimee.

"It's in China now, in what's called the Tibet Autonomous Region. Back then Lhasa was known as the Forbidden City. Outsiders were prohibited from going there, but David-Néel wasn't about to let that stop her. She was fluent in Tibetan and she figured she'd find a way to sneak in. She and a teenage lama named Aphur Yongden set out, with David-Néel pretending to be his mother. She put on traditional Tibetan clothing, blackened her hair with ink and darkened her hands and face with soot.

"It was winter in the Himalayans and the journey was arduous. They climbed nineteen-thousand-foot peaks without supplemental oxygen. There aren't many fifty-five-year-olds, men or women, who can do that. Twice they were almost robbed. They became stuck halfway across a raging river, suspended from ropes. They nearly starved to death when they were trapped in a mountain pass during a snowstorm.

"It took them two months to reach Lhasa. When her true identity was revealed the people there took her presence in stride. They decided she must have been returning to where she'd lived during a previous incarnation.

"David-Néel wrote a book about the journey that made her famous. By then she'd been away from Europe for a decade. Her return to France made newspaper headlines around the world. She published around thirty books about travel and mysticism and Eastern religions. Her books influenced writers like Jack Kerouac and Allen Ginsberg. She adopted Yongden as her son in 1929. They were together for forty years until his death in 1955."

Aimee wondered what all that had to do with anything. "That's interesting," she said. "Is there a point?"

Seamus went to his water dish and lapped noisily before settling down with a sigh at Aimee's feet. Aimee slipped off one of her loafers and rubbed her toes along the dog's shaggy side.

"The point is that I read about something she did and decided to try it," said Karen.

"What did you do? Did you adopt a teenage boy?"

"No." Karen went to the window and stood looking out. It was pitch dark outside and the window glass gave her back her own reflection. She stood there, unmoving, silently looking out. It made Aimee nervous.

"What did you do?" she asked again, more insistently.

Karen turned around. "I made a tulpa."

"What's that? Some kind of religious pilgrimage?"

Karen didn't answer at first. She sat down at the table and looked off into space. "As I said, Alexandra David-Néel studied with the Gomchen of Lachen. The local people were in awe of him. It was rumored that he could fly through the air, kill men with a glance and command demons. David-Néel claimed the Gomchen taught her to levitate. She also claimed to have learned the technique of *tummo* from him. It's a way to use one's internal energy to produce heat in order to withstand cold. She claimed that's how she and her adopted son were able to survive temperatures that fell to well below zero while they were crossing the Himalayans. Her detractors scoffed. They said she was lying, making up sensational stories in order to sell books, but I have reason to believe she was telling the truth."

She studied Aimee unblinkingly. "I saw things during my time in Nepal that were inexplicable. I saw an old monk produce a shower of purple and white crocuses out of thin air. They were real, thousands of them, flowers with stems and leaves still attached. They rained down around him until they formed a huge pile. I touched them. They were real. He invited me to take one and I have it still, pressed inside a book. It wasn't a trick or an optical illusion. I saw other things that seemed unbelievable, but they happened. It convinced me that people are capable of incredible feats if they put their minds to it.

"I decided to give it a go. First, I tried to levitate. I fasted and meditated, focusing every ounce of my will, thinking, *Rise! Rise!* I couldn't do it. All I got was a headache. I tried for days, giving it my all, but I couldn't manage to levitate a single solitary inch. Same thing with *tummo.* Nothing, no matter how hard I tried. I had better luck with the tulpa. That's the problem."

"You still didn't say what that is," said Aimee.

"The Tibetan word for them is *sprul-pa.* It means 'emanation' or 'manifestation.' It's an object or a being created through spiritual or mental powers."

Aimee was nonplussed. "You mean an object like that bowl?" She pointed to a ceramic bowl on the table filled with apples.

Karen nodded. "Yes, or even something like a person. Alexandra David-Néel claimed she created a tulpa that looked like a jolly Buddhist monk. She said it followed her around and other people could see it too. Think of it as an imaginary friend you can see.

"That's ridiculous," said Aimee.

"You think so?" Karen smiled tiredly. "I disagree. I made one. You saw it; it looks like a cowboy. I overheard the maids talking about it. I tried to unmake it, but I couldn't do it. It seems that it's harder to unmake them than is it to make them. Ironic, huh? Putting all that effort into creating one then realizing too late that it was a bad idea? I should have paid more attention to what David-Néel wrote about her tulpa getting out of her control. Now I'm afraid it's turned evil and it intends to harm to me and our entire family."

"That's crazy. The man who's been hanging around here isn't some kind of supernatural spook; he's just a vagrant."

"Then why hasn't the sheriff been able to find him?"

Aimee snorted. "Ewell Haskins couldn't find his own behind if he used both hands and a flashlight."

"Point taken," said Karen. "However I assure you the cowboy you keep seeing is no vagrant. He's not even a real person. I *willed* him into existence. I based his appearance on the cowboy actors my mother knew – Roy Rogers and Tex McGuffey and Smiley Burdette – guys like that. I met some of them when I was little and Mama took me to Los Angeles to visit her friends from when she was in B movies. Sunset Carson showed me how to twirl a lasso. I just about died from happiness.

"When I decided to make a tulpa, I thought about all those old-time movie cowboys. I pictured them down to the tiniest detail. After a long time it worked. I wish it hadn't."

Faint blue light had begun to brighten the kitchen windows. Birds were starting their morning routine, chirping and calling, as if to say, "Wake up! Let's get those worms!" Suddenly, behind the pebbled glass pane in the door leading to the terrace a form loomed up. It pressed its face against the glass, as if trying to see in. The doorknob turned. Seamus raised his head and whined.

"It's him," said Karen, standing up and looking wildly around. "It's the cowboy."

CHAPTER FIFTEEN –A GUEST OF THE FORMER PRESIDENT OF ULAKISTAN

The door opened and a man wearing a ten-gallon hat stood framed in the doorway. Karen and Aimee froze, thinking it was the intruder. Although Aimee wasn't convinced that Karen really had created a supernatural stalker there was something eerie about the cowboy with the wide, painted-on grin and his ability to seemingly appear and disappear at will.

Then they realized it was Marsh.

"Hello, you're up early," he said cheerfully, pocketing a set of keys. "I saw the kitchen lights were on and thought Louetta was making breakfast. I don't suppose you ladies have any coffee for a tired old cowpoke who just rode in from Texas?"

He did a double-take. "Karen? Is that you? My god, it is you!"

"Hi, Marsh," she said.

He pulled out a chair and sat down at the table. Seamus went over to him and Marsh scratched him behind the ears while he studied Karen through narrowed eyes.

"So you're not dead after all. I'm surprised Aimee let you in here after you attacked her in the swamp."

Karen looked at Aimee, who shrugged. "She forgave me. We're friends now," Karen said.

"Glad to hear it. Family disputes are tiresome. How about making me some coffee?"

"Make it yourself," said Aimee.

"All right," he said, getting up and opening cabinets. "I bet you wonder where I've been."

"Where *have* you been? I tried to get in touch with you," said Aimee.

Marsh found a canister of coffee in one of the cabinets. He pried off the lid and sniffed the contents, nodding in satisfaction. "Good and strong, the way I like it," he said. "I like to make coffee so strong that a spoon stands up in it. Sometimes my coffee is so strong it melts the spoon."

He proceeded to scoop a generous amount of coffee into the coffee maker. "I got your texts, but I chose to ignore them," he told Aimee. "I was too busy having fun with my old pal Andy in Texas." He turned on the coffee maker and sat down, waiting for the coffee to brew.

"Then why are you here now?" Aimee asked.

Marsh took off his white cowboy hat and tossed it across the room. It sailed through the air, landing neatly on one of the coat hooks next to the basement stairs. "Louetta texted me. Said some weirdo's been hanging around, scaring everybody. She sounded worried. I don't ignore Louetta's texts the way I do yours." He smiled at Aimee.

"What were you doing in Texas?" asked Karen, hoping to distract them from what threatened to turn into a quarrel.

"Riding and roping and target-shooting and cattle-driving and having a heck of a good old time. Andy has a huge spread out there. He's got a mechanical bull. I managed to stay on it for forty-five seconds. Andy said he doubted a professional rodeo rider could do any better."

The coffee finished brewing. He poured some into a ceramic mug bearing the image of a black arch with three fluted columns, symbol of Blanton's alma mater, the University of Georgia.

"Who's Andy?" asked Aimee. "Give me some of that coffee."

"I'd like some too, if you don't mind," said Karen. "We've been up all night."

Marsh got two more mugs and filled them with coffee. "Andy is what I call him. His real name is Andrej. He's the former president of Ulakistan. We got to know one another through business transactions I did with him involving the Ulakistani military. Andy's a swell guy, although his enemies would disagree. They call him the Madman of the Steppes. They're upset over some of the things he did during his rise to power."

"You're friends with someone called the Madman of the Steppes?" asked Aimee.

"Sure, why not? Live and let live, that's my philosophy."

Marsh brought the coffee-filled mugs to the table and set them down in front of the two women. "Do you ladies take anything in your coffee? Cream? Milk? Sugar? Karen, do you want some butter to put in yours? Isn't that how they drink tea and coffee in your part of the world? I'm afraid we don't have any yak butter. All we have is the kind made from cows' milk. Will that do?"

"Just sugar's fine," said Karen, reaching for the sugar bowl.

"How about you, Aimee? Do you take snake venom in your java? I know how you love your reptile friends." Marsh opened the refrigerator door and looked inside, pretending to scan the shelves. "Sadly, we appear to be out of that, too. I'll speak to Louetta about laying in a supply."

"You're hilarious," said Aimee. "I take my coffee black, like your heart."

Marsh stretched his arms above his head and yawned. "Somebody's grumpy this morning. Where was I? Oh, yes. Good old Andy. So when rebels stormed the presidential palace he managed to get on a plane and make it out of there, just in time. He said the rebels chased the plane down the runway in jeeps, firing rifles at it. It must have been very dramatic. Andy had anticipated the coup and took the precaution of transferring most of the money in the treasury to bank accounts in Switzerland and the Caribbean. Now he's a guest of the United States government. He's got a big spread in Texas, with a herd of longhorn cattle. He'll be staying there until the CIA or whichever government agency in charge of such things decides it's safe for him to go back to Ulakistan and retake control of the government."

"You keep getting mixed up with dubious characters. Aren't you afraid one of them will murder you?" asked Aimee.

Marsh spooned sugar in his coffee. "Not at all," he said placidly. "I've been shot half a dozen times – once by our former butler, as you know – and stabbed more times than I can count, but nobody's managed to kill me yet. I like to think that if I'm ever murdered, it's going to take a lot to put me down for good. I'm like Rasputin. He was hard to kill. As for Andy, he went in for murder on a large scale. One-on-one he's fine. He's a terrific host. Very generous. He'll give you the shirt off his back. He gave me that hat and these boots." He stuck out his foot to show off an ostrich-skin cowboy boot with a three-inch stacked heel and a silver toe cap. "Hand-stitched. The stones are genuine turquoise, set in silver. Nice, huh? When I wear these, I'm five-foot-seven. I feel like a giant. I could ask him to get you both a pair, if you want."

"They're not really my style," said Aimee. "And Karen's a nun now. She took a vow of poverty. I doubt she wants a pair of fancy cowboy boots."

"It's tempting, but I'll pass," said Karen.

"No kidding? A nun? Not many families can say they have both an arms dealer and a nun in them. It'll be interesting to see what Benjamin and Jubilee turn out to be," said Marsh.

The kitchen door opened and Louetta came in carrying a canvas shopping bag "It's not too bad out there yet," she said. It was how people in southern Georgia often begin conversations in the morning, before the temperature starts to creep up into the eighties, nineties and beyond. "It's been a warm fall. The radio said it'll be in the low nineties by noon, but right now it's bearable." She put the shopping bag on the counter. "I brought some peppers and tomatoes from my garden." Then she noticed that Aimee had company. "Mister Marsh! Thank goodness! And Ms. Karen! Thank the Lord! You ain't drowned after all."

Louetta had been told an abridged version of the drowning story, one in which Karen accidentally slipped and fell into the swamp and Aimee had tried and failed to save her.

"It's good to see you, Louetta. I'm a nun now. That's where I've been all this time, at a monastery in Mississippi," said Karen.

Louetta compressed her lips. "Is that more Buddhism? I would have thought you'd have gotten that business out of your system by now. Anyway, I'm glad you're all right."

She tied on her apron. "Omelets suit y'all for breakfast? I can put in onions and cheese and peppers and tomatoes. Sausage too, unless Ms. Karen can't eat that because of her Buddhism."

"No sausage for me, thanks. Everything else would be fine," Karen said.

Louetta regarded them, a worried expression on her face. She was usually unruffled. This nervous hesitation was unlike her. "I don't like bringin' it up, but I think Janelle and Anea are fixin' to quit,"

"Who are they?" asked Marsh.

"Two of the maids," said Aimee.

"Oh, well. We can always hire more."

"Maybe not," said Louetta. "Talk gets around. There's been talk about that crazy white man who hangs around here. The sheriff can't catch him. Janelle and Anea say he's not human. They say he a ghost."

"Nonsense," said Marsh.

Louetta reconsidered. "They both don't say he a ghost. It's Anea who say that. Janelle say he a serial killer, which is worse than a ghost." She began cracking eggs into a mixing bowl as Marsh and Aimee and Karen gaped at each other.

"Let's go in the breakfast room," said Karen, rising. "There's something Marsh should hear."

CHAPTER SIXTEEN – THE WRONG SHADE OF GREEN

The breakfast room had pistachio-green walls, accented by rectangles of white decorative molding framing wallpaper panels of green parakeets and yellow canaries perched among peony blossoms. The cypress floorboards were bleached a pale gray. Beneath the glass-topped white wicker dining table was a rug made of braided jute. Sunlight streamed in through French doors leading to the patio.

It was this pretty, cheerful room that was responsible for the death of Deidre Trapnell, mother of Marsh, Trainor and Aimee.

Deidre was originally from Rochester, New York. She was working as an investment banker in Manhattan when she met Blanton. Deidre was a blunt-spoken woman with an assertive (some would say frighteningly aggressive) personality. Life in the Deep South, where at the very least a veneer of politeness was expected from almost everyone, didn't agree with her. She traveled a great deal when her children were young, much to everyone's relief. When she was at White Oaks, she divided her time between bullying the servants, punishing her children, and redecorating.

In most cases her decorating efforts were an improvement. Deidre had a good eye for color and design. The breakfast room had originally been depressingly gloomy. Its single barred window made it seem jail-like, the bars having been installed long ago to prevent young female servants from sneaking out at night to meet up with their boyfriends. The walls were a cheerless blue-gray. A ponderous mahogany sideboard, dining table and uncomfortable Windsor chairs added to the unpleasant atmosphere.

Deidre had the barred window removed and French doors installed, allowing light to pour in. White-painted wicker furnishings from a shop on Tybee Island gave the room an airy San Tropez appearance. The transformation would have pleased her, except for one thing. She disliked the shade of green paint on the walls. She was crushed that it didn't match the sample the decorator had shown her.

Deidre responded to the disappointment by telephoning the decorator and screaming abuse at him. She point-blank refused to pay him for the work he'd done up to that point. The decorator later told people that Deidre had threatened to go to his shop and "get" him.

"What do you suppose she meant by that?" he asked, clearly rattled. No one could say because by then Deidre was dead.

After the tragedy, it was pointed out that it would have been easy for Deidre to simply choose another shade of paint. She might still be alive if she had.

Instead she phoned her friend Valerie, who had recommended the decorator to her. Deidre had hoped to scream at Valerie, but she got a busy signal. She kept trying for twenty minutes, getting a busy signal each time and getting progressively angrier. Finally, in a towering rage, she got into her red Aston Martin and sped off toward Valerie's house, intending to tell her off.

Through the center of Cobbs she went, at ninety miles an hour. People ran onto the sidewalks to watch as the Aston Martin roared by.

An old man seated on a bench in front of the barbershop noted her passage to the barber who'd come outside for a breath of fresh air. "There goes Deidre Trapnell. She's in a hurry. Probably on her way to give some poor bastard hell."

"Yankee women," said the barber, shaking his head. Those two words spoke volumes about his opinion of the female population north of the Mason-Dixon Line.

"She's a New York City Yankee woman, too; those are the worst kind," said the old man.

Valerie lived out in the country, not far from the golf course, on a street originally called Hog Haw Road. Its name was changed to the more pleasing Sassafras Drive when the subdivision where Valerie lived went up in the nineteen-sixties.

Driving like a fiend, Deidre tore along the narrow, two-lane road paralleling the golf course. If she had looked out of the window, she would have seen golfers moving across the greens. Preoccupied as she was with the prospect of ripping into Valerie she failed to look. If she had she would have seen that one of the golfers was Valerie, driving her signature pastel pink golf cart. No one else in Cobbs had a pink golf cart. Valerie's husband bought it for her for Christmas one year from a Dallas department store famous for its extravagant "his and her" gifts. His matching golf cart was baby blue.

Valerie had left her phone off the hook before lying down to take a nap. She forgot to replace it when she left the house. That's why Deidre had been unable to reach her.

The Aston Martin was capable of reaching a top speed of 155 miles an hour. It may not have been going quite that fast, but the police later estimated it was traveling at least one hundred miles an hour when Deidre came over a rise to find a pickup truck backing out of a driveway directly into her path.

Deidre was a good driver. She did the right thing. She slowly depressed the brake pedal, praying she wouldn't hit the truck. The Pirelli tires grabbed the road, leaving a smoking thirty-foot trail of black rubber. The Aston Martin lurched to a stop four inches from the side of the truck. There wasn't a scratch on either vehicle. The driver of the pickup stared down at her, wide-eyed.

Instead of thanking her lucky stars that she had avoided a collision, Deidre got out and advanced on the pickup, castigating the driver for not looking where he was going. She was heaping on the abuse when over the rise behind her came a sedan driven by a paper bag salesman on his way to the fertilizer factory.

Blanton owned the fertilizer factory. He was known for being a stickler for punctuality. Everyone later remarked how ironic it was that the salesman was in such a tearing hurry to be on time to meet Blanton at the factory that he didn't see the woman standing in the road until it was too late.

Looking around the breakfast room, Aimee said, "This is where we had the buffet after Mama's funeral. Daddy insisted on it. I always thought it was an odd choice, since she died because she got all worked up over the color of the walls. You never knew with Daddy. Was he being ironic or was he paying some kind of heartfelt tribute to her?" Aimee shrugged. "I guess we'll never find out. It turned out to be too small. People were packed in here, cheek by jowl. More were standing outside on the patio, waiting to get to the food and the bar. We should have had it in the ballroom."

Marsh cut into his omelet. "The floor's springy in the ballroom. It's marvelous for dancing, but it's not good for eating and drinking. Hillman was afraid something would get spilled and someone would slip and break a leg. Hillman was devastated by Mama's death. Funny how well he and Mama got along. Mama didn't like many people, but she was very fond of Hillman."

"We all liked Hillman, until he shot you and stabbed my husband to death," said Aimee.

"He was only doing what he thought was right," said Marsh. "I don't hold it against him. In fact I regularly send him commissary money. His sentencing's been delayed. They're keeping him in federal custody until he finishes telling the feds all he knows about that nasty business involving the sigul of Jörmungandr. If I know Hillman he'll spin it out for as long as possible. He's a cagey old fellow. Meanwhile Special Agent Burns and her colleagues are doing everything in their power to keep him contented while he names names. He's quite comfortable. Agent Burns assured me that the jail where he is isn't bad, as jails go. It's certainly nicer than some of the ones I've been in."

Aimee put down her fork, surprised. "You were in jail? You always told me you'd never been in jail."

"I qualified it by saying I'd never been in jail in this country. I've been locked up several times in other countries. Say what you will about American jails, they're like five-star hotels compared to some of the lockups I've been in. Ones in Venezuela and Rwanda spring to mind as being particularly unpleasant. Fortunately my stays there were brief, as I was able to bring about my swift departure either by engineering my own exit or by bribing the guards into leaving a convenient door unlocked."

Karen laughed. "Marsh, if I didn't know you better I'd swear you were making that up."

"If by that you mean that I've led a colorful life, during which I proved to be resourceful, thank you," said Marsh. "Getting back to Mama's post-funeral shindig, I thought the turnout was exceptionally good. There were cars parked all along the drive and along both sides of the road out front. They had to send two sheriff's deputies to direct traffic. I was surprised; I didn't think she had that many friends."

"She didn't," said Aimee. "People were scared not to go to her funeral or to the house afterward. Word got around that Daddy wrote down the names of everyone who signed the guest book at the funeral home."

"What do you mean?" asked Karen.

"I mean they knew there'd be trouble for anyone who didn't show up to pay their respects: loan applications refused at the bank, building permits denied, leases not renewed, memberships revoked at the country club, all sorts of things," Aimee said. She ate one of the grapes Louetta had added to their breakfast plates. "Remember Floyd Shelburne who used to run the hardware store? He didn't go to Mama's funeral. Not only was his lease not renewed, his daughter didn't get crowned Miss Fertilizer Factory in the Pecan Harvest parade that year, despite everyone saying she was sure to win."

Marsh and Karen silently considered that. "Well, this is a nice room. I think if Deidre had seen it like this, with the morning sun coming in, and the three of us having breakfast together, she'd be pleased," said Karen.

Marsh laughed. "I wouldn't count on it. I can't recall Mama being pleased about much of anything, ever."

Aimee poured herself more orange juice. "So listen to this," she said to Marsh. "Karen says the guy who's been lurking around here dressed up like a cowboy is some sort of spiritual manifestation called a tulpa. She said she created him. Isn't that the nuttiest thing you ever heard?"

Aimee expected him to laugh, but instead he looked thoughtful. "Those are hard to get rid of," he admonished Karen, as if she had been guilty of leaving food out and as a result they'd gotten roaches.

"Don't tell me you believe in them," said Aimee.

"I do, actually. Don't forget I've traveled extensively in the course of my profession. I've been to some peculiar places and seen some peculiar things. I believe tulpas exist."

Aimee opened her mouth to respond. Marsh held up a restraining hand. "Mind you, I've never personally encountered one, but I had it on good authority from one of my associates that they exist and are troublesome to get rid of. Unfortunately he's deceased, or I'd ask him more about it."

"Was that the same guy who told you he saw a yeti once?" asked Aimee.

"It's not; that was someone else, a well-known mountaineer. He's still alive, as far as I know, although that could change at any time, given the dangerous nature of his sport. Not that he'd be any help to us with ridding ourselves of a tulpa. He's been a guest on a number of television programs in which he talked about summiting Mount Everest and K2 and other inhospitable mountains, losing fingers and toes to frostbite in the process. You'd think that would put him off mountain climbing, but it hasn't. I asked him once what compelled him to do it, but he was unable to put it into words, poor fellow.

"It could be that he's more articulate when he's being interviewed on television. I wouldn't know because I never watch television if I can help it." He paused, seemingly stuck with a thought. "Did you know Aleister Crowley was a skilled mountain climber? Doesn't that seem an unlikely sport for a heroin addict to take up?"

Aimee shook her head. "I never heard of him."

"I have," said Karen. "He called himself the wickedest man in the world. You know *The Addams Family*? He was the inspiration for Uncle Fester."

In response to Marsh's blank look, she said, "It was a television show based on cartoons by Charles Addams. Children liked it."

"I'm familiar with Addams' work. His mordant sense of humor appeals to me. I wouldn't have thought it appropriate for children, however, but you never know with television. I've heard they make some very odd programs, including ones in which foul-mouthed young people are encouraged to indulge in reckless behavior for the entertainment of viewers. It seems ghastly, but from what I hear those sorts of programs are wildly popular." Marsh shrugged, mystified by what passed for amusement among the masses.

"As for Crowley, I'd wager he saw a yeti or two. The mountaineer I mentioned told me in confidence about seeing one. He said he may have been suffering from altitude sickness at the time, so he wasn't sure whether he was hallucinating or if he really did see it. I don't discount the idea that yetis exist, but since we're not dealing with a yeti but with what Karen claims is a tulpa, I think we should..."

He didn't finish saying what he thought they should do because Lee entered the room. He paused at the sight of Karen.

"Good morning," he said. "I see you have company. If I could have a word with Ms. von Helgern?"

"She's not company," said Aimee. "She's my stepsister Karen. She's not dead after all."

"I'm pleased to hear it," said Lee.

He turned to Karen. "Good morning, Ms. Trapell. It's a pleasure to find you among the living."

"Thank you," said Karen.

"She's a Buddhist nun now," said Aimee.

Lee placed his palms together at his heart and bowed. "In that case, namaste."

"Namaste," replied Karen, returning the gesture.

"What's up, Lee? You seem perturbed," said Marsh.

Lee cleared his throat. He looked over his shoulder toward the kitchen where Louetta was making mayonnaise. Her mayonnaise was a wonder, as were her grits. Not only skilled at down-home cooking, what Louetta called her "fancy kitchen-work" would have made Escoffier beam with approval. Luncheon that day was to be salmon en croute with Béarnaise sauce and haricots verts with almonds and caramelized shallots. For dessert there would be lemon crêpes filled with sweetened ricotta.

Lee lowered his voice. "It's the, er, the trespasser, sir. He's back. I passed him walking up the drive on my way in to work."

Marsh patted his lips with a linen napkin. Pushing back his chair, he rose to his feet. "How far up the drive was he?"

Lee paused to consider. "About a quarter of the way."

The crushed oyster shell drive leading to White Oaks was one mile long.

"And you got here when?" Marsh asked.

Lee consulted his wristwatch. "Five minutes ago, sir. I arrived at precisely seven-fifteen."

"Great! That means I can go out the back, circle around, and catch him unawares." Marsh rubbed his hands together. "I love catching people unawares."

"Be careful; whenever I've seen him he's worn a holster with two guns in it," said Aimee. "I don't know if they're loaded."

Marsh patted his abdomen, where a concealed-carry holster with a 9-millimeter Glock G43 nestled next to his appendix. "I have a gun and it's definitely loaded. I'll hold him at gunpoint until the sheriff arrives. If he tries to shoot me, he'll be sorry." He affected a cowboy drawl. "Folks say I'm the fastest draw west of the Pecos. I can skin that smoke wagon quicker than a bobcat can wink."

Karen wrung her hands together. "Please, Marsh. This isn't a joke. Don't confront it. It's not a human being; it's a tulpa. I don't know what it's capable of."

Marsh put his head to one side and smiled. "Is that so? Then let's see what happens. This should be interesting. I never shot a tulpa before, but if I have to I will."

He went into the kitchen and got his ten-gallon hat. He put it on, lowering the brim to just above his eyebrows. Whistling the theme from "The Good, the Bad, and the Ugly," he opened the French doors and stepped outside.

CHAPTER SEVENTEEN – BURN HOLE

Five minutes later Marsh stumbled back into the breakfast room. He was white-faced and trembling.

Karen gasped. Her hands flew to her mouth.

Marsh plopped down on one of the wicker chairs and put his head between his knees.

"Did you see him? What happened? Are you okay?" asked Aimee.

Marsh raised his head. "Do I look like I'm okay?"

"You look like you saw a ghost."

"I saw something, that's for sure. The damn thing zapped me. Look here!"

He pointed to the front of his shirt. There was a burn hole in the left sleeve.

"My favorite Enzo Merlungatti shirt, ruined," he said sadly.

"You've got dozens of shirts. Marsh, you scared the hell out of me. I thought something serious happened," said Aimee.

Marsh shook his head. Color was beginning to come back into his face. "Something serious did happen. You of all people should understand. You're a clothing designer. You must be aware that Enzo Merlungatti is universally recognized as a master of his craft. And now this shirt is ruined."

"So get another one."

"There are no other ones, not from Merlungatti's spring 2018 collection. This was my only one from that collection. It was my very favorite of all my shirts."

Marsh examined the hole. His voice rose in an affronted wail "This is a tragedy. I loved this shirt. I take good care of my clothes. I have the first bespoke suit I ever bought, after I graduated from Harvard. It's a beautiful thing, made for me by Andrew Hewlitt of St. James Street. It still fits perfectly. It's not as if I can go to Wal-Mart and replace this shirt. This shirt was special."

Aimee poured some coffee from the insulated carafe and passed the mug across the table to her brother. "Drink this; you'll feel better." She turned to Lee. "Mister Marsh is in need of a restorative."

"Coming right up," he said snappily. "I'll fetch something from the dining room sideboard. Perhaps the twenty-five-year-old Macallan would be appropriate under the circumstances."

The Trapnells watched as he left the room, bemused that the butler would have a suggestion for the right whiskey to drink after being attacked by a tulpa.

"Dare I say that Lee is becoming a treasure?" Marsh drank coffee and smiled. "He'll never replace Hillman, but he has a certain *je ne sais quoi.*"

Aimee shrugged. Except for her housekeeper and the herpetologist who took care of her snakes she paid no attention to servants, as long as they did what she wanted them to. "I forgot you went to Harvard."

Marsh made a face. "That's because Daddy didn't like to talk about it. He was ashamed of me going there. He wanted me to go to the University of Georgia, like he did. He was so put out by my choice of school that he refused to attend my graduation ceremony. He went to Trainor's graduation, though, from that third-rate cow college he eventually managed to matriculate from."

Karen was getting edgy. This airing of old resentments wasn't addressing the problem at hand. "What happened with the tulpa? You said it zapped you."

"Here's how it went down. I still can't believe it. I went outside with a light heart. It's a lovely morning, birds chirping, the sky the color of a flawless sapphire, the fountains in the gardens sending exuberant jets of water into the air. In general it was a fine morning on which to accost a trespasser.

"I was bright-eyed and bushy-tailed, primed for an encounter with the cowboy, be he mortal man or supernatural creature. I went around the side of the house and there he was, striding along the drive, headed for the front door. I crouched down and moved stealthily, thinking it would be a piece of cake. I'd draw down on him and order him to halt.

"As I reached for my gun he spun around and he fixed me with the creepiest stare I can ever recall encountering, and believe me, I've encountered some creepy stares in the course of my business. Before I could break leather, he raised an index finger and pointed at me. At first I thought a wasp stung me. It hurt like hell."

Lee reappeared with a bottle. "A restorative shot of whiskey in your coffee, sir?"

"Please."

Lee complied.

"What happened next?" asked Karen.

"I looked down and there was a hole burned in my shirt. My arm stung, as if I had received a nasty electrical shock. I could feel it tingling in the fillings in my teeth. I looked up and the crazy bastard was grinning at me. He held up his index finger and blew on it, miming a cowboy blowing smoke from the barrel of his gun. Then – and this is the weirdest part – he zipped backwards, fast as could be, like a fish that's been hooked and is being reeled in. He zipped down the drive and vanished out of sight."

"Now do you believe it's a tulpa?" asked Karen.

Marsh poured more whiskey in his coffee cup. "I don't know what to believe. No human being could do what I saw that thing do. I'm certain of that much."

Aimee drummed her fingers impatiently on the glass table top. "Okay, Karen. You said you willed the tulpa into being after reading what that lady wrote in her book. You said she got rid of the one she made. Did the book say how she did it?"

"No, just that it was hard to do. I thought I'd ignore it and eventually it would go away, but it didn't work. Then I tried willing it to go away, concentrating as hard as I could, but that only seemed to make it angry, as if it knew I wanted it to vanish. It seems that hard as it is to make a tulpa, unmaking one is even harder. Just as Alexandra David-Néel described, it started out seeming playful. The other nuns and monks at the monastery got a kick out of it. They went, 'That's a tulpa! Can you believe it! Karen made a tulpa.' It was making me conceited and vanity was something I thought I'd conquered."

Karen got up and looked out the French doors. The tension in her posture made it clear that she was expecting to see the cowboy outside, grinning at her. "It followed me around, popping up unexpectedly and grinning that spooky Cheshire cat grin. I kept thinking, 'go away, go away; go back to wherever you came from,' but it wouldn't. I started to feel a sense of menace emanating from it. I got the feeling that it wanted to hurt me and hurt my family. It scared me.

"The rinpoche at the monastery recommended that we perform a ceremony called *lhasang*. It involves calling on the various buddhas, bodhisattvas, and protectors for help in cleansing a negative force. It didn't work. That's why I left the monastery and came here. I wanted to apologize to Aimee for hurting her when she was little. I thought if I sincerely apologized I'd be cleansed of the wrongs I'd done and the cowboy would go away."

Marsh sighed. "I have a great deal of respect for Buddhism. I have a lesser degree of respect for Christianity, although I find the philosophy behind some of the ideas expressed in the New Testament laudable. Both religions have things to recommend them, but apparently tulpas can't be eliminated by acts of contrition."

He finished his coffee and twisted his neck from side to side, feeling the vertebrae pop. The encounter with the tulpa had confused and intimidated him. Marsh didn't like feeling confused and intimidated. "What I wonder is how did it manage to zap me? It wears two guns, but it didn't reach for them. Could it be they're just window-dressing? How could it shoot what felt like a bolt of electricity? It didn't use a stun gun; it simply pointed its finger and zapped me. If it can do that what else can it do?"

He got up and pushed his chair under the table. "If you ladies will excuse me, nature calls. I'll be right back." He left the room and headed down the short hallway leading to a powder room, his boot heels clicking on the cypress floorboards.

He paused to examine the collection of framed photographs lining the walls. The earliest ones dated from the mid-eighteen hundreds. They had been enlarged from daguerreotypes and the collodion positive photographs known as ambrotypes. Many of them featured White Oaks when the house was its original size.

Family groups stared grimly into the camera. Their bodies were held in the stiff, uncomfortable pose of people who have been warned not to move or blink. There were men holding the bridles of fine horses and ladies in hoop skirts. There was a scowling boy in a Lord Fauntleroy suit with a lace collar who bore an eerie resemblance to Blanton.

There were groups of servants. Slaves, Marsh reminded himself. They were lined up, looking every bit as uncomfortable as the white folks. There were the slave cabins which used to be where the conservatories were now. Chickens pecked in the dirt outside and black women and children stood in front. Their faces wore uniformly blank expressions, even the youngest children, as if they were thinking, *Get on with it. Take our picture and leave us alone.* Marsh's lips twisted in a grimace. "The peculiar institution," he muttered.

One of the photographs was of what Marsh took to be a blacksmith's shop. Its wide barn doors were open, revealing a forge and a collection of neatly arrayed tools. Whoever was in charge kept it in apple-pie order. Stacked outside were rectangular panels of ironwork. Marsh recognized the lacey filigree patterns of weeping willows and flowering vines that decorated the galleries at the front of the house. This must have been where they were made. Interested, he leaned in for a closer look.

Beneath a longleaf pine tree in the foreground stood a group of people, all of them black, all but one male. One of them, a heavily muscled fellow who wore a leather apron, Marsh presumed to be the blacksmith. The men were gathered around a woman. She wore an ankle-length gingham dress and was barefoot. On her head was a long strip of fabric folded into a head covering called a tignon. The fabric had a gleam to it that made Marsh suspect it was silk or satin. It was impossible to guess its color, but something told him it was a deep, rich red. In her hand she held a stick. The men's gazes were fixed on the ground where something had been scratched in the dirt, presumably by the woman with the stick.

The woman stared straight into the camera. She was young, no more than twenty, with a narrow face and high cheekbones. There was something unflinching and challenging in her gaze which intrigued Marsh.

"What could she be doing?" he murmured.

He couldn't make out what the woman had drawn in the dirt. Could it be the alphabet? Was she teaching the men to read? That wasn't supposed to be allowed, was it? Whatever she was doing, she was doing it openly, apparently uncaring of any retribution. Marsh wished he knew more.

CHAPTER EIGHTEEN –
A RELUCTANT LEARNER PROVES USEFUL

As Marsh exited the powder room, he heard a noise. It came from the end of the hallway where there was a set of doors leading to the *porte-cochère,* the covered area intended to protect passengers getting into and out of carriages in bad weather. One of the ornate brass doorknobs rattled. Someone outside was trying to get in.

Marsh took his gun from its holster and clicked off the safety. He crept to the doors and drew back the deadbolt. Then he stepped back, taking aim at what he gaged to be chest-high of whoever was out there.

"Come on in, you grinning freak," he shouted.

If he had been the type of nervous person who hears a strange noise in their house and opens fire, assuming it to be a burglar without checking first to make sure, the result would have been tragic. Since it was Marsh, who had virtually no nerves, he held his fire, waiting to see what the tulpa would do.

It wasn't the tulpa. It was his brother Trainor. He had a bright blue duffle bag slung over one shoulder. It had a picture on it of a cartoon character, an elephant wearing a monocle and spats and a derby hat called Sir Timothy Tuskaroo. Marsh recognized the bag as one Trainor used to take to sleepaway camp when they were boys.

Incensed, Trainor asked, "What's got into you? How come you were hollering? Hey! How come you're pointing a gun at me?"

Marsh holstered the gun. "I thought you were a tulpa. I was attacked by one a few minutes ago."

"You mean like the one that French lady, Alexandra David-Néel, made?"

Marsh couldn't have been more astonished if Seamus had spoken.

"What did you say?"

"A tulpa, like the one I read about in a book." Trainor put the duffle bag on the floor. A shirtsleeve flopped from the drawstring opening. The sleeve bore what looked like gravy stains. Marsh regarded it with distaste.

"I packed in a hurry," Trainor said defensively. "Palmer's on the warpath. I thought I'd better leave for a few days until she cools down."

"The two of you should consider getting counseling," said Marsh. "Getting back to what you said before, what do you mean you read about tulpas in a book? You don't read books. You don't read anything as far as I know, except for menus and labels on wine bottles."

"I don't read books *anymore,*" Trainor said, as if Marsh had accused him of indulging in some childish activity, like pretending to be a pirate or a superhero. "Why would I waste my time doing something like that?"

"Some people read for pleasure."

"They must be crazy. I only used to do it because they made me at St. Botolph's."

That was the boarding school Blanton sent him to after he'd failed eighth grade for the second time. Its full name was St. Botolph's School for Reluctant Learners. Trainor, a reluctant learner if ever there was one, had been induced to read by a program the school had called Reading is For Winners!

"They'd let you go in this room where they had video games like Pac-Man and Ms. Pac-Man and Chimp-Out Road Rage and Aztec Warrior Conquest. It was pretty cool, but they made you read a book before they let you play any of the video games. They checked to make sure it was a chapter book, not a comic book, a chapter book. Those are the hardest kind of books," Trainor said with a look of reminiscent horror.

"And one of the books you read was by Alexandra David-Néel?"

"Naw, it was by some guy. I don't remember his name. She was just mentioned in it. I only remember her name because there was a girl I liked named Alexandra, and I had two friends named David and Neil. It sort of stuck in my head. The book was called 'Remarkable Amazing Mysterious True Stories.' It wasn't too bad, as books go. It had stuff in it about UFOs and ghosts and people who disappeared, as well as the tulpa. I thought it would be cool if I could make a tulpa. I'd make one that looked like a hot girl."

"I have no doubt that you would. Now to what do we owe the honor of your presence?" Marsh removed the photograph that had intrigued him from the wall.

"Palmer's been at me to help her with this project she's all revved up about. She wants to build the *Titanic*. She won't quit yammerin' about it. It got on my nerves. I'm going to visit Peach Walker. The Coast Guard dropped the charges against him. He's got a new speedboat and he invited me to go with him when he takes it out for the first time. I thought I'd stop by here first and get somethin' to eat and pick up some clean clothes." He noticed the picture. "What are you doing with that?"

"I was going to show it to Aimee and Karen, to see if they know anything about it."

"Karen? You mean our stepsister Karen?"

"The very same."

"She's alive?"

"Alive and well. She's been in a Buddhist monastery in Mississippi all this time. She's in the breakfast room."

Trainor's bearded face broke into a grin. "Hot damn! We can take her to Judge Sparks and tell him the woman he saw was an imposter who was tryin' to steal our money."

"It wasn't an imposter. It was Karen. She gave him Daddy's will. She also claims she created a tulpa. It looks like a cowboy. Whoever or whatever he is, he zapped me with some kind of invisible energy beam. It ruined my shirt. See?" Marsh pointed to the hole burned in his sleeve.

"Big deal. I get holes in my shirts all the time," said Trainor. Indeed the bright yellow t-shirt he was currently wearing had a good-sized hole in the front. Written across the chest was BOBBY BODINE'S GOOD-TIME ROADHOUSE. HOME OF THE GIGANTO BURGER. I ATE THE GIGANTO BURGER.

"It's four pounds of hamburger meat, a pound of cheddar cheese, hot peppers, lettuce, tomatoes, coleslaw and dill pickles. I ate one," Trainor said proudly.

"Kudos on that remarkable achievement," said Marsh. He started in the direction of the breakfast room, the framed photograph under his arm. Trainor hurried to keep up with him.

"That's great news about the will. Wait until Palmer hears we're gettin' our inheritance. Listen, if you want to know about that picture I can tell you about it. I had to do a project in school about codes one time. Hillman showed me that picture. Then he took me upstairs and showed me the secret codes. I copied them down in a notebook and did an oral report. The teacher gave me an *A*. It was the only *A* I ever got."

Marsh halted. "What are you talking about?"

"The secret codes," Trainor said patiently. "You know the ones. They're on the front of the house."

"I have no idea what you're talking about. What secret codes?"

Trainor shook his head. "I can't believe you don't know about this. Daddy knew about it. He said it was why the house is still standing, despite the Yankees burning down plantation houses, and hurricanes and whatnot. Hillman said so, too. He said the codes are for protection. Are you sure you don't know about this?"

"What on earth are you talking about?"

"Come on. I'll show you."

Trainor poked his head in the breakfast room. "Hey, Karen. You're not drowned after all, huh? Marsh said you made a tulpa. That's awesome. Hey, Aimee. What's up?"

"We just finished breakfast," said Aimee. "I suppose you're hungry, since you're always hungry. Louetta can make you something."

"In a minute," said Trainor. "I'm taking Marsh upstairs to see the secret codes."

Aimee and Karen looked at him in puzzlement.

"Ha! You guys don't know about them either. Come on, I'll show you," said Trainor.

They went upstairs to the second floor and out onto the long balcony which ran across the front of the house. Below them the velvety green front lawn swept away into the distance. There was no sign of the tulpa.

Trainor was clearly delighted to know something his siblings didn't. He cleared his throat and assumed the lecturing tones of a tour guide.

"I draw your attention to the ironwork making up the railing in front of you. Note the weeping willows, the tangled vines, and the beautiful flowers, forming a sin...sin..."

"Sinuous is the word I believe you have in mind," said Marsh.

"Right. A sinuous design. Visitors to New Orleans have observed the same kind of decorative ironwork balconies on many of the old buildings in the French Quarter. Why, you ask? How did they get there? Who made them? I will tell you. Be prepared to be amazed, for the story is a strange one."

"For Pete's sake, Trainor, get to the point," said Aimee.

CHAPTER NINETEEN – ADINKRA

Trainor explained that the ironwork balconies in New Orleans were inspired by a mixture of French and Spanish architectural influences. Among those who apprenticed as blacksmiths in the Crescent City were enslaved black men from West Africa. They were primarily Ashantis from the Ashanti kingdom and Akan people of Ghana and Gyamen of Côte d'Ivoire. They had a complex system of symbols called adinkras, which they used in their fabrics and their pottery and their architecture to represent various concepts and aphorisms.

Trainor pointed to a shape worked into the trunk of one of the weeping willow trees in the white-painted iron railing. "See this here?"

"It's a heart," said Karen, leaning in to look more closely. "People carve them on trees, usually with their initials and the initials of someone they love. This one doesn't have any initials in it."

"That's because it only looks like a heart," Trainor told her. "It's really an adinkra called akoma. It means patience and tolerance. Hillman said so. This thing that looks like a fern?" He pointed to a shape with two loops on the bottom and what looked like a series of fronds on either side. "It's called an aya. It means endurance. There's all kinds of them here, if you know where to look. I guess the white dudes who hired the black dudes to make railings and other metal stuff didn't know about the codes. They thought they were just pretty designs. Hillman said there's some that are insulting, too. He said they were meant as a diss to white people for – you know – slavery and shit."

"That's interesting," said Marsh. "I wonder if the woman in the picture was drawing adinkras in the dirt for the blacksmith and his assistants to copy. But how would she know about them, and why would she be telling the men what images to put on the railings?"

"Probably because she was a Voodoo priestess," said Trainor casually. "Listen, I'm hungry. I'm goin' downstairs to get something to eat."

"Hold on! A Voodoo priestess? What do you mean?" said Aimee.

"I mean a Voodoo priestess. Duh! You know, like Marie Laveau, the one in the song about how she'll put a spell on you? She was a big deal, back in the day. People still visit her tomb and leave offerings. They make Xs on it in chalk, asking her to grant their wishes. Her tomb's above ground, the way they are in New Orleans because of the high water table. It's got Xs all over it. I saw it when I was there one time."

The others looked at him, wondering what could have caused him to visit the tomb of the woman known as the Voodoo Queen of New Orleans. It seemed like an unlikely thing for Trainor to do. They soon got their answer.

"A bunch of us went there for Mardi Gras. It must have been twenty years ago now. It was Peach Walker and Griff Hathaway and Earle Fine and Hoss Detweiler and me and some girls we knew. We had Hurricanes at Pat O'Brien's and then we had Pimm's Cups someplace else and then we had Hand Grenades at the Tropical Isle. Griff Hathaway got his wallet stole when he was walkin' down Bourbon Street; at least that's where he thought it happened. Peach got beer thrown on him. A panhandler spit on my shoe."

"That is exactly why I refuse to go to Mardi Gras," said Marsh.

"You're missing out," Trainor told him. "Mardi Gras is fun. I wish they had it all the time. One of the girls we were with, Cecily Pernell, heard about the making-an-X thing on Marie Laveau's tomb. She bought a piece of red chalk from a guy who was sellin' it outside the cemetery and she made us all go in with her. I don't know what her wish was, but if it was to marry Earle Fine, it came true and boy was she sorry later! My point is Voodoo is real. Hillman said – and Daddy backed him up on this – that they used to do it right here, in this house. That's what the teeth and chicken bone doodad in the tin box Daddy kept in his office was all about."

He turned, about to go downstairs, when he was struck by an idea. "If you want to get rid of the tulpa, you should ask a Voodoo priestess for help. Fight supernatural fire with supernatural fire, you know? Hillman said there's one around here, but he wouldn't say who it was."

Aimee gave an exasperated sigh and brushed a strand of hair off her forehead. "Voodoo in Cobbs? Trainor, that's absurd. There couldn't be somebody here who practices Voodoo. If there was we would have heard about it. That's not something they'd be able to keep quiet. They sacrifice chickens and goats and have big bonfires in the woods and beat drums. No way is anything like that happening around here."

She laughed and shook her head. "Who do you think is the Voodoo priestess? Birdsall Gormley? Edith Felcher, over at the library? I can't picture either of them dancing naked around a bonfire, can you?"

Edith Felcher was a prim woman who ran the library with an iron fist. A book returned with dog-eared pages earned permanent revocation of the offender's borrowing privileges. Edith owned many cats and was fanatically devoted to playing a sport called pickleball. Her enthusiasm for pickleball led to her mounting a campaign to have it included in the Olympics. So far she had been unsuccessful, but not for lack of trying.

"Hillman was putting you on. He may have been right about some of those designs in the ironwork being old African symbols, but that doesn't mean anything, no more than the Hex signs Pennsylvania Dutch farmers have on their barns mean anything. It's just folklore. There's no such thing as magic. Cobbs is boring. The most exciting thing that goes on around here is Bunco Night at the Masonic Temple," Aimee rolled her eyes to show what she thought of Bunco Night. "This isn't New Orleans. There are people in New Orleans who pretend to be Voodoo priests and priestesses, but it's just for fun, to entertain the tourists. They have shops where you can buy love charms and goofer dust and mojo bags but they're fakes, made in China. They don't have any power to do anything. Voodoo's not real."

"How do you know?" asked Karen.

"Because it's not."

"That's not a valid argument," said Marsh.

"Don't tell me you believe in it?" Aimee said.

Marsh opened his mouth to speak, but she cut him off. "I know what Voodoo is. It's sticking pins in dolls."

Karen went to the railing and rubbed her hand over the weeping willow with a heart in its trunk. "I suppose you think Buddhism is doing yoga and chanting 'om.' There's much more to it than that. There are more things in heaven and earth than are dreampt of in your philosophy."

Aimee looked at her, perplexed.

"That's a quote from *Hamlet,*" Marsh told her.

"You know, Shakespeare," said Trainor helpfully. "He lived a long time ago. He wrote a bunch of plays. I heard some of them have dirty jokes in them."

"Hold thy peace, thou knave," Marsh told him.

"What?" said Trainor.

"Never mind," said Marsh. "Go on, Karen. Tell us what you think."

"I've done some reading on the subject," Karen said, folding her arms. "Did you know that in Benin and Haiti, Voodoo is officially recognized as a religion? There are people here in this country, some of them highly educated people, who practice it. They consider it to be a religion as valid as any of the mainstream religions. To them, Voodoo is a way or life, a set of guiding principles, the same way Buddhism is to me. That's Voodoo with a capital V. Then there's voodoo with a lower-case V. That's the kind where people stick pins in dolls to let off steam at somebody they don't like. Or they burn money-attracting candles the same way they buy scratch-off lottery tickets, not really expecting to get rich, doing it just for fun. See the difference?"

"Yes, but what do we do now?" Aimee asked. "The tulpa or whoever he is exists. The sheriff couldn't catch him. Marsh couldn't shoot him or capture him or whatever he was going to do before he got zapped. So how do we get rid of him?"

"I told you," Trainor said patiently. "You weren't listening. We find the Voodoo priestess and get her to help us. Now I'm goin' downstairs. I'm hungry. While I'm down in the kitchen, I'll ask Louetta if she knows who the priestess is."

That was a bad move. Louetta was highly insulted.

"I am a deaconess at the Mount Pisgah AME Church. There is no way I would mess with that sort of thing," she said. "Reverend Macomber will vouch for me. He knows I would never mess with devil worship. I'm shocked you'd suggest such a thing, Mister Trainor. Shocked!"

She bowed her head. "Shocked!" she whispered.

Janelle and Anea were seated at the kitchen table, observing the interaction between Trainor and Louetta with interest. Janelle had a bowl of vinegar and water and was using it to clean the crystal prisms from the chandelier in the dining room. Anea was idly peeling a hard-boiled egg while watching something on the little flat-screen TV Louetta kept in the kitchen.

Anea got up and hugged Louetta. She cast a reproving glance at Trainor. "He didn't mean to hurt your feelings, Louetta. He just thought that since you a woman of color you'd know a Voodoo priestess."

Louetta threw off Anea's embrace and gave Trainor a horrified look. "Really? Is that what you think of me? You think I associate with devil worshippers?" Her voice rose to a shriek. "Is that what y'all think?"

The Trapnells stood there, shocked and speechless.

Louetta untied her apron and flung it on the floor. "I am leaving this house forever," she announced dramatically. "I refuse to stay here one more minute and get insulted. I put up with a lot from y'all, but this time y'all have crossed the line."

It took considerable apologizing and pleading from all four Trapnells before she agreed to stay.

"I guess y'all are overwrought by that cowboy ghost or devil or whatever he is that goes sneakin' and peepin' around here, puttin' everybody's nerves on edge," she told them. "Go see Reverend Macomber. He a man of God. He'll know what to do. In situations like this, it best to go straight to a man of God, not to some nasty, devil-worshipping Voodoo priestess." She shook her finger at them to drive home her point.

CHAPTER TWENTY –
THE TEMPTATION OF REVEREND
MACOMBER

Martin Macomber, Doctor of Philosophy in Pastoral Ministry, presided over a small, white vinyl sided church on a cul-de-sac at the end of Jackson Avenue. It was about twenty feet away from the railroad tracks. Beyond the tracks was the road leading out of town. There was no longer any passenger service to and from Cobbs, but freight trains rattled by noisily about once an hour. When that happened the entire building shook. As a result, worship services at Mount Pisgah AME Church had to pause until the racket subsided.

When the Trapnells stopped by to speak with the pastor, a long freight train bound for Tallahassee thundered by just as they entered his study. They stood there, smiling awkwardly at each other, for a full two minutes until it passed and quiet reigned once again.

"Welcome. Please be seated," Macomber said when it was finally quiet. He had the confident voice of a man who is used to being instantly obeyed. His chubby face creased in a smile as he shook their hands. He gestured to a group of chairs upholstered in nubby plaid fabric. He was young, in his early thirties, a recent seminary school graduate with a wife and two children.

"Mister Trapnell, I can't tell you how grateful we are to you for your generous gift," he told Marsh.

"It was nothing," Marsh said.

"Oh, ho-ho! Nothing, he says! I don't call a new roof nothing. Do you?"

He looked to Aimee and Trainor and Karen for confirmation that a new roof was indeed something.

"Nope," said Trainor. "A new roof ain't nothing."

Macomber smiled roguishly. "Not only a new roof. A new roof *and* a new organ. That was Mister Marsh Trapnell's extremely generous gift to our congregation, wasn't it, hum?"

He looked at Marsh, eyebrows raised inquiringly.

"Yes," said Marsh miserably. He hated having his generosity remarked upon. "But really, there's no need to thank me. I was happy to help."

"Ha!" said Macomber. He lunged and punched Marsh playfully on the arm. Unfortunately it was where the tulpa had zapped him and his arm still hurt. Marsh winced.

"Look at him!" Macomber chortled. "Look at how modest he is! It pains him to admit that he came to our aid, unasked, in our time of need. If we didn't replace the roof, this old building would have been done for. Water would have poured in like the Biblical flood, sweeping us all away. It would have been like the parting of the Red Sea up in here. We would have been like Pharaoh's army, chariots, soldiers, horses, and all, washed away!"

He spread his hands, letting them picture the congregation being swept away in a mighty tide, church ladies in fancy hats, men in their best suits, little children, all swept out the door, over the railroad tracks and out of Cobbs.

"What's more, with that broke-down old organ wailing like a sinner in Satan's clutches the choir couldn't raise their voices properly in song, making a joyful noise unto the Lord. Now with the new organ Mister Trapnell got us they sound like the heavenly choir! Ha-ha! And he calls it nothing!"

He gazed down at Marsh and shook his head, *tsk-tsking* in mock disapproval. "Don't tell me not to thank you. I am going to give thanks where thanks are *due*." He punctuated the last word by punching him again in the same spot.

"You're welcome," Marsh gasped, rubbing his arm.

Macomber seated himself behind his desk and folded his plump, well-tended hands. "So, Louetta Waites tells me you folks have a problem. We set great store by Ms. Waites here at Mount Pisgah. She's in charge of our Tiny Tots Testament Storytime Hour and our Mother's Day program and our Bountiful Harvest for the Hungry food pantry. She does a splendid job. In my opinion no finer Christian woman walks the earth, with the possible exceptions of my dear wife and my dear mother."

He looked at the Trapnells, as if challenging them to suggest a better example of Christian womanhood than Louetta Waites. They nodded respectfully.

"She bakes good cakes," Trainor offered.

The pastor rolled his eyes to the ceiling, on which sprayed-on fire retardant formed little white peaks resembling whipped cream. "Oh, Lord! Her cakes! Don't tell a soul but..." He lowered his voice to a hushed whisper. "One time I ate an entire one of her caramel cakes all by myself. I wish I had one right now, as a matter of fact. Gluttony is a sin; I'm aware of that, but oh my! Ms. Waites' cakes! They tempt me the way Delilah tempted Samson. I am powerless to resist Ms. Waites' cakes."

"As are we all," said Marsh. He cleared his throat and leaned forward. "Pastor, we've got a problem out at White Oaks."

"Ah! I'm sorry to hear it. Does it have anything to do with Mister Blanton's will? There have been rumors that all was not as it should be, staggering debt, foolish investments, women claiming to have given birth to his secret children. Things of that nature. There's a rumor that the property is being sold and will be turned into condominiums or a Wal-Mart Superstore, not that I like to repeat such things, you understand."

He waited, brown eyes gleaming behind the lenses of his eyeglasses. It was obvious he expected to hear them disclose something juicy about their father, whom the townspeople had respected and feared but didn't much care for as an individual.

"Nothing like that," Aimee said firmly. "My stepsister Karen here has created a tulpa." She nodded at Karen, who nodded back.

"It's true. If I'd known what they're like, I wouldn't have done it, but now it's here and it won't go away," Karen said. The pastor stared at her, amazed.

"So anyway," said Aimee briskly. "We want to find out if you know a Voodoo priestess who can make it go away."

Macomber studied them, eyes narrowed. Then he grinned. "Oh, I get it! This is one of those internet challenges. Tell a man of the cloth something outlandish and see how he reacts. That's it, isn't it? You really had me going there for a second. Am I on camera? Are you filming this so you can put it up on YouTube?"

He smiled, eyebrows raised expectantly, waiting for them to produce a camera. Then his face fell. "You're not joking, are you?"

"No, we're serious," said Karen.

Macomber sighed. Aimee's t-shirt – one of her Clobber designs – had deeply unsettled him. On the front was a picture of a hideous beast holding up a human rib cage. Written beneath it was LET ME LOVE YOU. What did that mean? What would make someone put something like that on a garment? He didn't know. He didn't want to know.

He examined his fingernails, trying to think of the best way to phrase the question. "Please don't take this the wrong way, but have you been experimenting with mind-altering substances?"

"No. We don't do that," said Aimee. "Trainor used to, but he doesn't anymore."

"That's right," said Trainor. "I used to, but my current wife won't allow it."

"I'm pleased to hear it, but seriously? You actually expect me to believe..." Macomber's voice rose as he struggled to get control of himself. He took a crisp cotton handkerchief from the breast pocket of his pale yellow button-down shirt and blotted his forehead. "Okay. Whew. Okay. Let's go over this, shall we? You claim to have created a supernatural being called a tulpa. Is that right?"

"Karen did. The rest of us had nothing to do with it," Aimee said.

"And now you're asking me to give you the name of a Voodoo practitioner in order to banish it, is that right?"

"Yep, you got it," said Trainor.

"What in the blue blazes makes you think I know a Voodoo practitioner?"

"Dunno," said Trainor. "My Daddy said there used to be Voodoo done at our house. Hillman said so, too."

Macomber looked even more dismayed. "Ah, yes. Hillman Parks. He was a member here for many years, since long before my time. I never would have believed he would have done what he did. Never in a million years. A sad case, very sad." He turned to Aimee. "You have my sincere condolences on the loss of your husband, but just because there may have been such, um, *activities*, in the area at one time, it doesn't mean that it still goes on. Not here. Not in Cobbs."

"That's what Louetta said. She got all worked up over it when we asked her if she knew a Voodoo priestess," said Trainor.

"I imagine she would," said Macomber. He stuffed the handkerchief in the pocket of his chino trousers. "You have to understand how Voodoo is viewed by some. It's thought of as a primitive religion, involving cannibalism, orgies, infant sacrifice and other horrors, practiced by savages. To African-American ladies of Ms. Waites' generation the suggestion that she would be involved in it, even to the extent of merely knowing someone who was a practitioner, would be taken as a dreadful insult."

"You've studied it, then," said Marsh.

"Of course. We studied its history in seminary school. There are aspects of Roman Catholicism in it, as well as ancestor worship. The various loa, the belief system, we studied all that. It's quite fascinating, but I'm sorry to say I don't know of anyone around here who practices it. I wish I did. I'm sorry I can't be of more help."

The Trapnells were downcast. Macomber had been a longshot. They didn't know who else to turn to.

The pastor cleared his throat. "Perhaps what you need is an exorcism. I have never performed one. However the Good Book says that any believer can cast out demons. I am a believer. A tulpa seems to me to be similar to a demon, if not an actual demon. If one is troubling your household, I could confront it and attempt to send it back to wherever it came from."

The Trapnells brightened.

"Great! Can we call you the next time we see it?" asked Aimee.

"Um, the thing is..." Macomber removed his horn-rimmed glasses, wishing he hadn't spoken so hastily. He took a little cloth from his desk drawer and proceeded to polish the lenses, stalling for time while he gathered his thoughts. "The thing is I've never done an exorcism. I think I'd need permission from the bishop. Then I'd have to study up on how to do it. That would take time. My wife is expecting again and I have to help out more at home. Our eldest keeps getting ear infections. The doctor says she's going to need tubes put in. She already screams bloody murder when we take her to get shots. I can't imagine how she's going to react to ear tubes. On top of that, my duties here keep me occupied, day and night. Not that I'm complaining, but..." He looked down at his hands clenched on his desk blotter. "I'm sorry."

"That's all right. We understand," said Marsh. "We'll figure something out."

Macomber got up and shook their hands. "I'll pray for you," he said.

CHAPTER TWENTY-ONE – SPECIAL AGENT BURNS' BIRTHDAY PARTY IS INTERRUPTED

It had gotten warmer outside while they were meeting with Pastor Macomber. A hot wind made a foaming sound as it gusted through the pine trees beyond the railroad grade crossing. Iron gray thunderheads bunched in the sky. A freight train rumbled past, headed north.

The Trapnells got into their father's white 1959 Rolls-Royce Silver Wraith and stared glumly at the boxcars tagged with graffiti rolling past them as fat raindrops splattered the windscreen.

"Well, shoot. There goes that idea," said Trainor. He turned the key in the ignition and switched on the wipers. He pulled the car to the railroad crossing, waiting for the train to pass. "You guys want to take a ride over to Pontahatcha? Get some ice cream?"

Trainor loved driving the Silver Wraith. He'd been dropping hints that he'd like to be given ownership of it once their father's estate was settled. "Here's what we do," he'd suggested. "We each make a list. We write down which things we want of Daddy's, in order of most to least, then we compare them. What do you say?"

"We already know what your list is going to say. It's going to say you want Daddy's car and all the paintings in the Gentlemen's Parlor," Aimee told him.

"Daddy didn't make any specific bequests in his will," Karen reminded them. "It would be easier if he had. He said he wanted his assets divided equally among the four of us. We can't cut the Rolls into four pieces."

Marsh laughed. "Maybe we could make a game of it. Sort of a quiz show. Whoever answers the most questions correctly gets first crack at the loot.

We can get Lee to ask the questions. We could dress up in formal attire and do it in the ballroom. We could invite the townspeople. It would be fun."

"I'd be at a disadvantage. I'm not good at answerin' questions," Trainor grumbled.

Aimee wouldn't mind owning the classic automobile. "How do you know? Maybe the questions would be ones you'd be good at answering. One might be, 'What's the best way to talk a prospective bride out of a prenuptial agreement?' Or 'What are five good ways to commit money-laundering, according to Peach Walker?' Those are the kind of questions you'd be good at answering."

"Very funny," Trainor said. "Why don't we ask Judge Sparks how we should divide up Daddy's things?"

The freight train passed and the gate went up. The car's tires bumped as Trainor drove across the railroad tracks and onto a narrow two-lane road grandly called the Cobbs-Pontahatcha Magnolia Highway.

"Judge Sparks is senile," said Aimee. "You might as well ask the old man who sells bait worms to Gordon Buzzy what he thinks, the one with the long white beard and crazy eyes. You'd get a more sensible response out of him."

Gordon Buzzy was the proprietor of Buzzy's General Store, a low-slung, ramshackle wooden building perpetually teetering on the edge of structural and financial collapse. If it didn't sell products that weren't available at the local Publix, such as chewing tobacco, bait, pickled pig's feet, and (secretly) moonshine whiskey it would have gone under long ago.

It began to rain harder. As they rounded a curve in the road, a figure sprang out from among the trees and darted directly in front of them. Trainor slammed on the brakes. The big car skidded, its tires screeching. The Rolls crashed into a ditch filled with weeks and muddy water. There was a loud *thud* as it hit the bottom of the ditch. The engine stalled.

Through the passenger side windows they could see the figure turn and grin at them. It was the tulpa.

"Damn it!" Trainor muttered, cranking the ignition.

"Don't! You'll flood it," Karen warned him.

Too late. The ignition made a clicking sound and then silence. The engine wouldn't turn over.

"Double-damn it! We're stuck in this ditch," said Trainor. He pounded on the steering wheel in frustration.

Something moved through the weeds, something long and green, with knobby skin. "Oh, look," said Marsh. "There's an alligator. It must live in this ditch."

The alligator wasn't large, as alligators go – about four feet long – but it didn't seem like a good idea to get out of the car. It was raining hard. The Trapnells sat there watching the alligator as it watched them.

"At least the tulpa's getting wet," ventured Karen.

"I don't think it minds being wet," said Marsh.

The figure was walking along the shoulder of the road, away from them. Every so often it turned around and waved.

"Do you have your gun? Can you shoot it?" Aimee asked Marsh.

"It's too far away. I doubt I could hit it from here," said Marsh. He took his phone from his pocket and examined the screen. "No bars. There's no cell service out there. We're stuck in this ditch with an alligator until somebody comes along. Wait a minute! I've got a signal."

They waited breathlessly while he placed a call for a tow truck to the garage in Cobbs. That done, Marsh called another number. It rang twice and then someone answered.

"Hello," said a voice on the other end.

"Hey there, Special Agent Burns! It's your favorite confidential informant," Marsh said cheerfully.

Carson Burns sounded less than pleased. "What do you want, Bad Choices?"

"Is that music I hear? It *is* music! Someone is singing karaoke, and quite badly by the sound of it. I can make out the sound of voices raised in convivial conversation. If I'm not mistaken, it's the sound of law enforcement agents engaged in revelry. Could it be that my favorite FBI agent is having a soirée and she neglected to invite me? I'm devastated."

"Bad Choices, please believe me when I say that I can't think of any circumstance that would induce me to include you among the people I would invite to a party."

"You wound me, Special Agent Burns, you really do. Did you get the case of Champagne I sent?" Marsh turned to his siblings with a smile.

There was a long pause. Then Burns' voice came over the phone's speaker. "That was from you?

"Yes indeed. Happy birthday."

"How do you know it's my birthday? How did you find out my home address?"

"I'm fiendishly clever. You know that," Marsh said.

"You're stalking me. It's a federal offense to stalk an FBI agent."

"I doubt sending you a case of Veuve Clicquot Yellow Label Brut Champagne would be considered stalking, but if it displeases you, send it back."

"I already opened it. My guests have drunk several bottles," Burns told him.

"In that case, let's move on, shall we? I need a favor," said Marsh.

Agent Burns groaned. "I should have known. I should have realized that Champagne was from you. Who else do I know who can afford a case of expensive Champagne? I was having such a good time, too, until now. What do you want?"

CHAPTER TWENTY-TWO –
A CALL FROM A FEDERAL PRISON

Later that afternoon Aimee found Marsh sitting in a rocking chair on the balcony outside the bedroom he used when he was at White Oaks. He was scanning the grounds behind the house with binoculars.

"That's a big gun you've got taken apart in there," said Aimee, motioning with her head to the room behind them.

"It's a Bellini Lupo bolt-action hunting rifle. I'm cleaning it," said Marsh, looking through the binoculars.

"What are those books on your desk? They're written in a strange language with curly letters."

"That's Sanskrit."

"You read Sanskrit?"

"Doesn't everyone?" Marsh lowered the binoculars and smiled tiredly at her. "Princess Farah sent them by overnight courier. They're hundreds of years old. They're from her collection."

"Isn't that the lady who lives in a fortified compound in Iceland, the one who collects erotic books and art?" Aimee had been there when Marsh arranged to send the princess a nervous, high-strung librarian from the UK named Cyril Chern-Humley. Their father had hired him to inventory the books in the library at White Oaks and then fired him in a fit of rage.

"That's the one. Not all of her collection is steamy. The books on my desk are about mysticism. The princess was grateful to me for sending her Chern-Humley. She said he was invaluable in inventorying her collection, particularly the netsuke. Apparently he really warmed to the task. I thought he might."

Marsh placed binoculars on the candlestick table beside his chair and stretched his arms over his head. "The princess is the last of her line, daughter of the former Shah of Ishran. The rest of her family is dead, killed by assassins, mostly. She's a lovely person. Educated at the Sorbonne. A charming hostess. One of the best conversationalists I've ever met. I don't get to see her as often as I'd like, since she refuses to leave her compound for fear of being assassinated and I don't often find myself in Iceland."

"You know some unusual people," said Aimee, thinking of Marsh's other friend, the Madman of the Steppes. "What are the books for?"

"I'm reading about tulpas, not that I'm convinced that our friend is a tulpa."

"You're not? Then what is he?" Aimee sat down in a rocking chair next to her brother's and put her sneakered feet up on the porch railing. The thunderstorm earlier had cooled the air. A pair of bats swooped from the eves, plummeting and pirouetting. In the distance an owl hooted.

"That's a good question," said Marsh. "Here's another good question: how much do you trust our stepsister?"

"Karen? Why?"

"Because her story seems fishy to me; this whole tale about renouncing material wealth and becoming a Buddhist nun. Does that seem like the Karen we know?"

Aimee thought about it. "Not really, but people change. Maybe she had some sort of spiritual awakening."

Marsh's lips quirked in a one-sided smile. "Like Saul on the road to Damascus? It has been my experience that people don't change, not in any profound sense. And how well do we know her?"

"Not that well," Aimee admitted. "She's a lot older than us. Maybe we'd see her once or twice a year." She stared at Marsh excitedly. "How do we know she's really a nun? She shaved her head, but that's not proof."

Marsh raised his hand for quiet. He picked up the binoculars and was watching something through them. "Just a deer," he said after a moment, lowering the binoculars. "Something was moving near the tree line, but it was only a deer." He crossed his legs, fussily straightening the crease in his trousers. "She really is a Buddhist nun. I contacted the abbess at the monastery in Nepal where she said she took her vows. It checks out. Karen really is a nun."

Aimee was irritated. "Then why did you question it?"

"I question everything. That's how I am. And here's another question: what do you know about that monastery in Mississippi where she was staying before she showed up here?"

"Nothing," Aimee admitted. "What is there to know?"

"The man in charge has an unsavory background. He's called Dorje Rinpoche, rinpoche being an honorific title meaning 'precious one.' He's thought to be from Nepal originally, although that's not certain. What is known is that he spent many years there. He had ties to the CIA, if my information is correct. He was rumored to have done a brisk business in drug smuggling and loan sharking and all sorts of naughtiness. Despite that he somehow managed to be granted a visa to come to this country. He became a naturalized American citizen in 1991. Since then he's presided over a community of monks and nuns outside of Natchez. Ostensibly he's a peaceful seeker after enlightenment. I wonder what he's really up to."

"You mean is he like Maharishi-what's his-name, the one the Beatles went nuts over before they decided he was a fraud? Do you think he's up to no good?"

"I don't know, but he seems too good to be true: a former criminal who became a holy man. And here's another question: how do we know the cowboy actually is a tulpa? We only have Karen's word for that. I've been reading about them in those books the princess sent. There's no firm evidence that they exist, just anecdotes from questionable sources. What it the cowboy's not a tulpa? What if he's a human being? Say, for example, that he's a stuntman. That would explain how he could contrive to move strangely and appear and disappear seemingly at will. Karen's mother was an actress. She knew people in Hollywood. Maybe Karen knows a stuntman and she hired him to pretend to be a tulpa."

Aimee hadn't thought of that. She'd assumed Karen had been telling the truth when she said she'd conjured a tulpa through prayer and visualization. "Why would she do that?" she asked.

"For the obvious reason: money," said Marsh. "She told us she thinks the tulpa wants to harm her and the rest of our family. What if she's planning to kill us in order to inherit the whole of Daddy's fortune? She could claim she had nothing to do with it; that it was a tulpa."

Aimee looked toward the darkened balcony of the guest room next door. Karen was staying in there. The curtains were drawn across the French doors and there were no lights on inside, as far as she could tell. Where was Karen? They'd left her in the Gentlemen's Parlor, talking to Trainor. Could she have crept upstairs and opened the doors a crack so she could listen to what she and Marsh were saying?

"That's too far-fetched. The police would never believe it," Aimee said.

"You're right. I don't see the police as being likely believers in tulpas. I doubt most police investigators have ever heard of them. Police tend to be rationalists. They're trained to think most murders are committed either for monetary gain, or for revenge, or because of sexual jealousy. Their natural assumption would be that Karen was behind it if you and I and Trainor were to be murdered, due to our deaths making her the only surviving beneficiary of Daddy's estate. However, if Karen is in league with a shady holy man, she could say that she doesn't want her inheritance, using the fact that she's taken a vow of poverty to back it up. She'll say that she's donating it all to the monastery in Natchez, to carry out their good work.

"If monetary gain is no longer an issue, the police would turn their attention elsewhere. Then Karen and the shady holy man would be free to split the money. Daddy's estate is worth forty billion dollars, by best estimate. People have killed for far less."

Marsh's forehead creased as he thought it over. "Saying it out loud like that, it doesn't seem feasible. It's too elaborate. Generally it's best to keep things simple when planning a crime. If Karen wanted to kill us, there would be easier ways of going about it than pretending that a tulpa did it."

He picked up the binoculars and scanned the property behind the house. "I don't know what to think. I still can't figure out how the cowboy managed to shoot a bolt of electricity at me. He could have palmed a small stun gun, I suppose. I didn't see any sign of a weapon but something zapped me and ruined my favorite shirt."

Not that again, thought Aimee. "The whole shirt's not ruined; just one sleeve has a hole in it. You could cut both sleeves off and wear it unbuttoned over another shirt."

Marsh lowered the binoculars and gave her a look of horror. "Cutting the sleeves off an Enzo Merlungatti shirt would be an act of desecration. I'm shocked that you'd suggest such a thing."

The sleeves were neatly rolled to the elbows of the shirt he had on, a paisley print in subtle shades of brown and blue, made of Sea Isle cotton. Like all of Marsh's clothing it fit him perfectly.

"That's a nice shirt you're wearing now," said Aimee.

Her brother regarded her mournfully. "You're trying to cheer me up. Thank you, but I'll mourn the loss of that particular shirt until the day I die."

His phone rang. He looked at the screen and brightened. "This is the call I was waiting for. Special Agent Burns has not failed me."

He turned on the speaker. Aimee could hear a recorded woman's voice: "You have a prepaid call. You will not be charged for this call. This call is from an inmate in a federal prison. Hang up to decline the call, or to accept, press five now."

Marsh pressed five. "Hello, Hillman," he said.

There was the sound of hacking coughing, followed by a familiar raspy voice. "Hello, Mister Marsh."

"How are you, Hillman?"

There was more coughing. Hillman's lung problems had worsened since he'd been taken into custody. "I'm tolerable. Thank you for the commissary money. How y'all doin' at White Oaks?"

"We're fine. We miss you," said Marsh.

Aimee made an outraged face. She mouthed *He killed my husband!* Marsh shook his head at her and mouthed back, *Let me talk to him.*

There was another deep, rattling cough, followed by the sound of Hillman blowing his nose. "You're too good to me. After I shot you and all. Sorry about that, by the way."

"No need to apologize. These things happen. Listen, we have a situation brewing at White Oaks. We might need the help of a Voodoo practitioner. Trainor said you told him one time that you knew of one."

There was a long pause before the old man responded. "I couldn't rightly say. Mister Trainor and I had that conversation a long time ago, back when he was a boy. He was doin' a project for school. I told him about the adrinkas in the ironwork on the balconies in front of the house. He did a school report on them and got an A. I remember how happy he was about that."

"Your memory is as sharp as ever, Hillman."

"Yes sir, Mister Marsh. I always did have a good memory. So does my granddaughter, Kortney. Her twin sister Kortnessa has a good memory too, but it's not in a class with Kortney's. You ask Kortney about a movie she saw years and years ago, and she can repeat most of the lines from it, word for word." He coughed again, a deep, bronchial cough. When he caught his breath he said, "Like I said, that conversation with Mister Trainor was many years ago. I don't know of anybody who would be of help to you now. I'm sorry, I wish I did."

"That's all right. It's not important. It was just a thought. Is there anything I can do for you, Hillman?"

"You've done plenty already. Thank you."

"All right then. It was good to hear your voice. I'll follow the progress of your case with interest. Goodbye." Marsh ended the call. He put the phone in his pocket and rubbed his hands together. "Bingo!"

Aimee looked puzzled. "What do you mean? He didn't tell you anything."

Marsh smiled, looking like a cat that has swallowed a canary. "He told me the name of the Voodoo priestess."

"No he didn't." Then Aimee's mouth fell open as she realized something. "Why, that sly old man! He knew the call was being recorded. He didn't want to say anything straight out that might get her in trouble so he went at it sort of sideways, didn't he? Telling but not telling?"

Marsh laughed. "Hillman always was the soul of discretion. In this case he was protecting the reputation of a member of his family. I doubt the regional board of education would be pleased to learn that one of the teachers at the high school is a Voodoo priestess."

CHAPTER TWENTY-THREE –
RICKY STUMPF FINALLY SNAPS

At breakfast the next morning Trainor was in a chipper mood. The garage in town had found nothing wrong with the Rolls-Royce after pulling it out of the ditch.

"Those old Rolls are like tanks. They're indestructible," he said, sprinkling a liberal amount of hot sauce on his grits.

Marsh drank espresso, tossing it back in one go, the Italian way. He replaced the tiny cup in its saucer. "That's true. My friend Andy owns several. He had the bodies armored and bulletproof glass installed and special armored plating put underneath to prevent being blown up by a bomb. He had to leave them behind when he fled Ulakistan one step ahead of the rebels. If and when he returns to power the rebels had better have taken good care of his cars or they're going to be sorry."

"Who's Andy?" asked Trainor.

Aimee cut into her French toast. Louetta made it with pecans and bananas and raisins, using Texas toast. Like everything she made it was sublime. "He's homicidal tyrant from a former Soviet bloc country."

"You've got some disreputable friends, bro," Trainor told his brother.

"Look who's talking. Peach Walker isn't exactly a Boy Scout," said Marsh. "Weren't you on your way to visit him? How come you're still here?"

"He texted me and said now's not a good time. He's lying low. He thinks the moving and storage company's under surveillance. He and his mom went someplace until it blows over. I thought I'd stick around here and see what happens with the Voodoo priestess," Trainor said. He spooned a heap of grated cheddar cheese on his grits and dug in.

Aimee and Marsh had informed Karen and Trainor about Kortney McNamara, their former butler's granddaughter, being a Voodoo practitioner. It was a Saturday, so the high school where she taught wasn't in session. They planned to go to her apartment later to see if she'd agree to help them banish the tulpa.

Marsh and Aimee had come to the conclusion that Trainor, unreliable in almost every way that counted, had an uncanny ability to come up with solutions to problems that baffled better minds than his. If Trainor thought a Voodoo priestess could help, then his siblings were willing to give it a try.

"What will we do if she refuses?" asked Karen. Despite having come out of hiding and sleeping in a real bed for a change she looked exhausted.

"We'll cross that bridge when we come to it," said Aimee. Her phone rang, showing a number with a 716 area code. It was Benjamin's school.

What now? She thought. She had a sinking feeling that Benjamin had run away or been expelled. It was what usually happened when he was at school.

It was the headmaster. Benjamin had not run away. Instead he had prevented Ricky Stumpf, a groundskeeper at the school, from burning the place to the ground.

Aimee sat there, amazed, as the headmaster, a man named Gilbert "Woody" Furlong, described what happened.

"Benjamin is safe. All the boys are safe, thanks to your son's quick thinking," Furlong told her. "Stumpf has always been moody. He's gotten worse since his wife filed for divorce. We knew he was going through a rough patch, but we didn't dream he'd do what he did. Apparently he's been drinking quite a bit. Not on school grounds, of course," he added hastily.

"Of course," said Aimee. She suspected Furlong was afraid of a lawsuit if word got out that the unstable groundskeeper had been drinking on school property.

"He worked at the school a long time. I can remember him puttering around, cutting the grass and raking leaves back when I was a student," Furlong said.

Aimee was aware that the headmaster was a graduate of Rayburn, what was known as an old boy. During her visit to the school on Homecoming Weekend Benjamin had gleefully shown her a photocopy of a page taken from the 1998 yearbook featuring Furlong's senior portrait. The future headmaster looked off pensively into the distance. He appeared to be thinking deep thoughts and contemplating great deeds. Beneath the picture was a quote from Henry David Thoreau. It said, "Go confidently in the direction of your dreams. Live the life you have imagined."

The boys had been busy with the photocopy. They'd given Furlong vampire fangs and a towering beehive hairdo. Neatly printed in a speech bubble above his head was, "Sportsmanship, gentlemen! Sportsmanship! It is the key to success in life, as well as on the playing field." It was a phrase he used often when addressing the students.

According to Furlong, who would have been outraged if he'd known of the existence of this unflattering portrait, Stumpf had snapped. He was fed up with the spoiled young scions of the wealthy that made up the student body. He was fed up with their expensive clothing and perfect teeth and the way that everything had been handed to them on a silver platter. He'd had it up to here with the teachers, who chummily chatted to him about sports and what kind of gas mileage he got on his truck. He could tell they thought they were doing him a favor by shooting the shit with him about the Philadelphia Eagles and the Fliers, which they assumed someone they thought of condescendingly as a blue-collar worker or a manual laborer or some other snotty term meaning a man like himself would care about. In truth, Ricky couldn't give a shit if the entire roster of both teams and every one of their coaches and fans were eaten by bears. He resolved to show them. He brooded about it for a long time before hitting upon a plan of action.

Stumpf's plan of action involved a can of gasoline and a box of wooden matches.

The field house was the first to experience the wrath of Ricky Stumpf. He used his master key to unlock the door then splashed the floor and the walls with gasoline. That done, he struck a match. It had been a dry autumn and the field house, GO RAYBURN RAMS! written on the green asphalt shingles of its roof in red block letters, went up with a loud *whumpf!* Next Stumpf turned his attention to the scoreboard. Like the field house it was made of wood. A few splashes of gasoline from his trusty red can and it, too, burned merrily when he lit a match.

Stumpf had prepared for his raid by drinking an entire bottle of tequila. He staggered as he went to his truck for a second can of gasoline. It was this he intended to use on the main school building, starting in the basement, next to the furnace. Once Old Main, as the building was called, burst into flames, Stumpf expected the neighboring dormitories would catch fire.

It was 3 a.m. The boys were asleep, tucked snugly in their beds, no doubt dreaming of becoming CEOs and Wall Street moguls and senior partners in law firms and other varieties of rich assholes. The dorms were equipped with smoke alarms and sprinklers, but in the ensuing chaos Stumpf hoped that at least some of the brats would perish.

He giggled as he stumbled to his truck, picturing the pandemonium that was about to ensue. Twice he slipped and fell to the ground, laboriously hoisting himself to his feet each time. His blue jeans were caked with mud, as was his flannel shirt. He'd left his ratty old sheepskin jacket at home and it was a cold night, but Ricky didn't care. He was having a very good time.

Under his breath he sang the Rayburn Fight Song. The first verse went: "Onward sons of Rayburn! Show them what you've got! Fight men of Rayburn! Ye shall fail not! Down the field to victory the Rayburn Rams shall trot. Fight! Fight! Fight! For the red and white!"

The other verses were even worse. The fight song was the creation of a slight, bespectacled boy named Percy Stillwell. Percy had been head monitor, debate club president, glee club president, editor of the student newspaper *and* the yearbook, chairman of the Greek and Latin Classical Society, captain of the baseball team, and much, much more. Percy was not only a high achiever he was popular with his peers, judging by the many accolades from his schoolmates who chipped in to donate the water fountain inscribed with his name which was installed in Old Main in his honor after he died in the influenza pandemic of 1918.

Percy didn't live long enough to graduate. As a consolation prize he was awarded a diploma posthumously and the school officially adopted his song.

Stumpf didn't know it but not all of the boys were asleep. One was awake and was watching him intently from the window of his darkened room. The boy opened the window, being careful to do it as quietly as possible. He fetched a long PVC tube from under his bed and loaded it with a projectile, tamping it down firmly into the barrel of the tube with a piece of sawed-off broomstick. Next he unscrewed the cap at the end of the barrel and sprayed hairspray inside the shorter piece of PVC which served as a combustion chamber. Quickly replacing the cap to hold in the hairspray he raised the homemade cannon so that it pointed out the window. When the giggling arsonist was within range, the boy inserted a barbecue lighter into a hole in the pipe and lit the flame.

"Geronimo," he whispered.

The result was immediate and gratifying. Out of the tube shot a good-sized Idaho potato. If flew through the air, striking Stumpf in the head, knocking him unconscious and breaking his jaw.

"Gotcha!" the boy said happily.

The boy was none other than Benjamin Monteleone, former troubled teen turned hero. Aimee was flabbergasted as the headmaster, his voice trembling on the verge of tears, praised him.

"We owe Benjamin a debt of gratitude. If it wasn't for his quick thinking who knows what might have happened?" he said.

"Is the man he shot going to be all right?" Aimee asked.

Furlong snorted dismissively. "Him? He'll be fine. Don't concern yourself about him. They've got him in the county lockup. The school will be closing ten days early for the Thanksgiving holiday in order to get things cleaned up here. When we reopen after the vacation we'll have a brand-new field house and a new scoreboard, an electronic one. It's being donated by the parents of one of the students." Furlong paused and cleared his throat portentously. "The board of trustees has voted to name the new field house after Benjamin, with your permission, of course."

"That's fine with me, if it's okay with Benjamin. Where did he get the potato cannon anyway? Are they legal?"

It turned out that Benjamin made it himself, using materials from a local hardware store. He'd volunteered to do it as an extra-credit project for chemistry class. "It demonstrates the basic principles of Boyle's Law," Furlong explained, "Under constant temperature, the volume of gas is inversely proportional to the total amount of pressure applied. And yes, they're legal in Pennsylvania. Benjamin made sure to ask first."

"I see," said Aimee. This was a new, law-abiding version of her son. It would take some getting used to. "I wonder where he got the idea to make one?"

Her gaze fell upon Marsh, who quickly looked down at his eggs Benedict.

Aha! Good old Uncle Marsh. If you want to know how to weaponize a potato, he's the man to ask. Honestly, this family! thought Aimee.

"He probably got the idea from the internet. That's where young people get their ideas nowadays," said Furlong.

Marsh was busily cutting his English muffin into bite-size pieces, a small smile on his handsome face.

"When can we expect you to come and get Benjamin?" Furlong asked.

"I've got my hands full right now. Tell him to go to New York. He can take a train or a bus and stay at my place on the Upper West Side."

A shocked silence followed this suggestion. Furlong cleared his throat. Sounding intensely uncomfortable he said, "Ms. von Helgern, I understand that you spend much of your time in Europe. Things in Europe are different than they are here. More relaxed, shall we say. Do you really think it's wise for a boy his age to travel alone to New York City?"

The way he said it made it seem as if Aimee had suggested that Benjamin should parachute into Afghanistan.

"Benjamin is eighteen. He's traveled by himself many times. He'll be fine. Tell him when he gets to the Dakota to be sure and ask Joaquim how the cobra is."

Furlong had no idea what to make of that. He knew the Dakota was a cooperative apartment building overlooking Central Park, one of the most desirable addresses in the city. He knew Aimee owned an apartment there, but the rest made no sense. "Joaquim? Who is Joaquim?"

"He's my herpetologist. I got him from the Bronx Zoo. He lives in a suite of rooms in the apartment across the hall from the one where I live. The rest of the apartment is taken up by my collection of snakes," Aimee told him. "I have a large collection of snakes. Fortunately it's a spacious apartment so there's plenty of room for them.

"Seventy days ago my favorite cobra laid eggs. She's an albino *naja naja* from Bangladesh, six feet in length and a lovely pearlescent pink in color. I want Benjamin to see how she's doing. The eggs should hatch soon. If they hatch while he's there I want him to be sure and send me a video. I love it when little snakes pop their heads out of their shells for the first time, don't you?"

"Sure," said Furlong gamely. "I love seeing that."

A compromise was reached. Benjamin would travel to New York in the company of another Rayburn student, Michael Hong, and his parents. The Hongs lived on Park Avenue, between East 71st and 72nd Streets. They'd deliver Benjamin to the Dakota. Aimee assured Furlong that her housekeeper would take charge of him from then on.

"Have a happy Thanksgiving, Ms. Von Helgern," said Furlong. "I suppose you'll be sharing it with Benjamin in Manhattan? Perhaps you'll be taking in the parade?"

Anyone who knew Aimee knew she despised large, public events. She would be the last person to stand outside in the cold in Midtown Manhattan being jostled by the crowd. That the headmaster suggested it showed how uneasy he was about allowing Benjamin to rattle around alone in an apartment. Furlong hoped for confirmation that Aimee would be there to keep an eye on her son and make sure he was in at a reasonable hour. Leaving him in the care of a housekeeper seemed negligent. What if Benjamin decided to go to a nightclub? One with flashing lights and pulsing electronic music and drugs? Furlong had heard lurid accounts of things called "raves." From what he understood some of the exuberant attendees would get so caught up in the music and the strobing lights that they danced until they collapsed, like victims of medieval dancing plagues.

"Maybe," Aimee said vaguely. "There are things going on here in Georgia that may take some time to resolve. We'll see. Have a happy Thanksgiving. I'm glad your school didn't burn down."

What a strange woman, Furlong thought as he hung up.

Trainor looked up from dipping a piece of bacon into his grits. "Benjamin's school almost burned down?"

"Somebody tried to set it on fire. Benjamin stopped him," Aimee said.

Trainor shook his head. "Why would he do a dumb thing like that? I used to wish my school would burn down."

Aimee turned to Marsh. "You taught my son how to make a dangerous weapon."

To his credit, Marsh didn't deny it. Instead he shrugged. "The world can be a dangerous place. It's best to be prepared should danger arise. Let's finish up here and go visit the Voodoo priestess."

CHAPTER TWENTY-FOUR –
BEGONIAS AND POLTERGEISTS

"How come we're bringin' her a flower? Is that what you're supposed to do when you go to see a Voodoo priestess? Is it some kind of ritual offering?" Trainor asked. He and Karen and Aimee and Marsh were in the lobby of Kortney McNamara's apartment building. Next to the buzzer for apartment 2C was a label on which was neatly printed the name K. McNAMARA.

Karen carried a potted begonia from one of the conservatories at White Oaks. She had on her wig and wore black yoga pants and a teal blue short-sleeved knit shirt. She was in disguise, she's told the others earlier, thinking it best to blend in with the locals rather than wear her Buddhist robes. She brushed a fleck of dirt from the begonia's clay pot and told Trainor, "It's what you're supposed to do when you visit someone's home. It's polite."

"Really? Who says? I just show up. Nobody ever said you're supposed to bring a plant. Are you sure you got that right?" Trainor asked.

"It's called a hostess gift. It doesn't have to be a plant; it could be any small, thoughtful item. It could be something to eat or drink," Karen told him.

Trainor turned to Aimee, dubious. "Is that true?"

"Yes, honestly Trainor, sometimes you act like you were raised in a barn," said Aimee.

Karen pressed the buzzer for apartment 2C. On the landing above them a door opened. Kortney appeared at the top of a flight of stairs covered in oatmeal-colored low-pile carpeting. "Hi, come on up," she said.

The Trapnells, curious as to what a Voodoo priestess' lair was like, entered her apartment.

Kortney NcNamara was a long-limbed, pleasant-faced woman. She taught mathematics at the consolidated high school, as well as coaching the girls' field hockey team. She seemed comfortable in her own skin. The Trapnells had never imagined she did anything more outré than reading the daily horoscopes. Yet if Marsh's interpretation of what her grandfather said in the telephone call was correct, she was a Voodoo practitioner.

They looked around her living room, finding it disappointingly conventional. The furnishings were the kind that came from Pottery Barn, attractive and functional. On the walls were colorful framed travel posters. There were no masks on display, no drums, no painted and feathered fetishes, no sinister carved wooden figures. It was an innocent room, spotlessly clean and sunny, smelling pleasantly of some kind of citrus-scented cleanser.

Kortney exclaimed over the begonia. "It's lovely, but you didn't have to bring me anything."

"See?" said Trainor. "She said we didn't have to bring her nothin'."

"We're trying to teach Trainor some manners," Marsh confided to Kortney.

"It's good to have manners. That's what I tell my students, not that they listen," she replied. "May I offer y'all some iced tea?"

"If it's not too much trouble," Karen said.

"She already said she'd give us some. How would it be too much trouble if she already said she'd do it?" said Trainor. Then he caught on. "Oh! I get it! That's manners." He frowned. "Seems like a lot of beating around the bush to me. If somebody asks if you want somethin' and you do, you should go, 'yeah, gimme some.' If you don't you go, 'naw, I don't want none of that.' It's quicker that way."

Marsh was examining the books in Kortney's bookcases, taking volumes out and leafing through them. He noted that among them were books by Freeman Dyson, J.B. Rhine, William Roll, Neil deGrasse Tyson, Guy Lyon Playfair, Mary Rose Barrington, Oliver Lodge, William James, and Brian Josephson.

Marsh turned to his brother with a smile. "You know, I think you're on to something there. You should write a book called *Gimme Some: Trainor Trapnell's Helpful Rules of Etiquette.* People would find it refreshingly blunt. It might even become a best-seller."

"You think so?" said Trainor. "I guess some people must read books. Kortney's sure got a lot of them, but she's a teacher. Reading's a job requirement."

Kortney returned with their iced tea. "Thanks for being good to Paw-Paw Hilly, sending him commissary money after what he did," she told them, using her pet name for her grandfather. Her face clouded. "I still can't understand why he did it. I've thought about it and thought about it and it doesn't make sense. He wasn't a violent man. It wasn't like him. I almost hope it'll turn out that he has a brain tumor, like the University of Texas tower gunman. Isn't that awful? At least that way there'd be a reason for why he did what he did."

"I understand your feelings and I sympathize," Marsh said. "I spoke on the telephone with your grandfather recently. He said you might be able to help us with a problem we're having."

"I'll do whatever I can," Kortney said.

"That's good to hear." Marsh turned from the bookshelves and leveled his cool gray gaze at her. "We're being stalked by a tulpa. We need to make it go away."

"A tulpa? Are you sure it's not a poltergeist? I always thought they might be one and the same," she said.

"Interesting," said Marsh. He sat down and crossed his legs. "Would you care to tell us why?"

"Have y'all heard of the Bell Witch?" Kortney asked.

"I saw a movie about it. She was a ghost that could turn into animals and stuff. That's totally freaky," Trainor said.

Aimee felt left out. It annoyed her that Trainor knew more about the subject than she did. "I saw the movie *Poltergeist*, but I never heard of the Bell Witch," she said.

"It was a series of paranormal events that took place in Tennessee in the early nineteenth century," Kortney told her. "Nobody knows how much is fact and how much is folklore. What's certain is that it wasn't a witch in the usual sense. It called itself a spirit. Andrew Jackson was said to have had an encounter with it before he became president. The story goes that he was on his way to visit the Bells when his wagon suddenly refused to move. There didn't seem to be anything wrong with it, but the horses couldn't budge it. Jackson excitedly called out that it was the witch's doing. From out of the air he heard a woman's voice answer him, saying she'd let the wagon move on and would see him that night. Then the wagon started to move again."

"That's creepy," said Karen.

"It is," Kortney agreed. "Jackson is said to have declared that he'd rather fight the entire British army single-handed than face the Bell Witch again."

"Gosh, and he was tough, too. He fought duels all the time," said Trainor.

"Personally, I think the part about Jackson encountering the witch was made up. He never mentioned it in any of his writings," Kortney said. "Andrew Jackson was one of the most famous people in America at the time. Saying he had a run-in with the Bell Witch makes the story seem more authentic."

Kortney got up and removed a book from the bookcase. "Here's a recent book about it. The author says she read through the old documents, including eyewitness accounts from friends and neighbors of the Bells, and from surviving Bell family members. Many of those were recorded years after the events at the Bell farm, so there's no telling how accurate they were. She came to the conclusion that something paranormal happened, but she's skeptical about the more sensational aspects of the story, including the part about the witch murdering John Bell."

"What? They said a ghost killed somebody?" Aimee said.

"If it was a ghost, it wasn't a conventional one, what's called a residual haunting. That's where an image of a dead person is seen but it doesn't interact with the living. Whatever the Bell Witch was it spoke and moved objects and interacted with people. The story goes that it tormented John Bell, and to a lesser extent, one of his daughters. Bell got gradually weaker and then died. He was supposedly poisoned by the contents of a mysterious bottle which was left at his bedside.

"The daughter, a girl named Betsy, got slapped by invisible hands and had her hair tied in knots. She broke up with the man she was going to marry on the witch's insistence. It begged and begged her not to go through with it until she broke off the engagement."

Kortney handed the book to Trainor. He nervously examined the illustration on the cover of a log cabin with a ghostly figure hovering over it, long, claw-like fingers outstretched.

"It's interesting that one of the causes for the haunting was said to be that John Bell or a member of his family had disturbed a Native American burial site," Kortney told them. "It keeps getting brought up as a reason for why locations are haunted. The late parapsychologist Hans Holzer used it all the time. So did ghost hunters Ed and Lorraine Warren, although the Warrens were more likely to blame supernatural disturbances on demons. They were devout Roman Catholics, so it's understandable why they'd view it that way."

"You know a lot about the supernatural," said Karen.

"I take an interest in it," Kortney replied.

"Is that because you're a Voodoo priestess?" asked Trainor.

CHAPTER TWENTY-FIVE – KORTNEY'S DOUBLE LIFE

Aimee choked on her iced tea. "Trainor!" she sputtered.

They looked at Kortney apprehensively, bracing themselves for her angry reaction.

"Subtlety isn't Trainor's forte," said Marsh, rising. "I apologize if he offended you. Perhaps we'd better leave."

"That's all right. I'm not offended. Sit down," said Kortney. "Anybody want more iced tea?"

"I do," said Trainor. "You got anything to eat?"

"Oh my god, Trainor. That's so rude," said Aimee. "Kortney, I'm sorry. We've never been able to domesticate him."

Kortney smiled and smoothed her braids. "That's perfectly fine. I have oatmeal-raisin cookies. They're from the bakery, fresh this morning." She left the room and returned with a plate of cookies and a pitcher of iced tea in which lemon slices floated. She put them on the coffee table and seated herself, folding her hands.

"It's true that I'm a practitioner of Voodoo, what some call Voudon. I don't advertise it. People who need to know are aware of it. Those who don't stay uninformed." She gave a laugh. "I guess you could say I lead a double life: high school teacher by day, Voodoo practitioner by night. It's better if I keep my religion on the down low. Some people have the wrong idea about what Voodoo is. You know what I mean?"

"We understand," said Karen. "I'm a Buddhist nun. Before I came here, I was staying at the Peaceful Place monastery outside of Natchez. I keep quiet about my religion when I'm in Cobbs. People here are conservative. If you're not a Southern Baptist or an Episcopalian or something like that they view you with suspicion."

"What is Voodoo, anyway?" Trainor asked.

"We believe in a supreme being called Bondye. Bondye created the world but doesn't get involved in human affairs. That's where spirits called loa come in. They're sometimes called *mystères* or 'the invisibles.' Followers of Voodoo call upon loa to act as intermediaries to Bondye. Each loa is responsible for a specific profession or activity. They can be called upon to help," Kortney said.

"It sounds like the way Catholics pray to Saint Christopher or Saint Jude," said Marsh.

Kortney agreed that it was similar. "For instance, say you're in love with somebody and they don't love you back. Followers of Voodoo would turn to Erzulie Fréda, the spirit of love. They'd offer her things like sweet cakes, pink Champagne or a gift of perfume or jewelry."

Aimee clapped her hands. "I like that!"

"So do I," said Kortney, smiling. "Loa can manifest by possessing the bodies of worshippers. We believe in a universal energy, and that the soul can leave the body during dreams. There's much more to it, but those are the basics."

"Where'd it come from?" asked Trainor. "Don't it come from New Orleans?"

"Not originally. Originally it probably came from West Africa, specifically Benin. The word 'Voodoo' means spirit in the Fon language. It might have evolved from ancient traditions of ancestor worship and animism."

"You lost me there," said Trainor.

"Animism is a belief that plants and inanimate objects and geographical features such as rivers and mountains have souls," Marsh told him. "It can be found in Native American religions."

"So how did it get here all the way from Africa?" asked Trainor.

Kortney sighed. "Kidnapping victims brought it with them, people who were stolen from their homes and enslaved, forced to work on plantations. They managed to keep many of their traditions and words from their languages."

The Trapnells considered that uneasily. Kortney hadn't said, *forced to work on plantations like yours,* but that's what she meant.

"That's terrible," said Karen. "I'm so very sorry."

Kortney nodded, her face solemn. "The diaspora was terrible. Its effects are still being felt today. It was an awful, awful thing. Anyway, getting back to what I was saying, the kidnapped Africans brought their religion with them. The Voodoo practiced today in this country and in places like Haiti has Christian overtones because slaves were forced to accept Christianity. In Haiti it was Roman Catholicism. Slave owners were given eight days for slaves to agree to become Roman Catholics. If they didn't the slave owners would have to pay a fine. They did as the law demanded and they weren't particularly gentle about it."

"This gets worse and worse," said Aimee.

"Some slaves only pretended to convert. They took their traditional religious beliefs underground and the old and the new got blended together. They'd display images of Catholic saints and pretend to be praying to them, but secretly they were praying to loa. For instance, in Haitian Voodoo, Saint Peter is Papa Legba, gatekeeper to the spirit world."

"Cool. It's like a secret society," said Trainor. "I was in a fraternity in college. We had ceremonies. Voodoo's like that."

"It's nothing like whatever hijinks you and your oafish fraternity brothers got up to. I shudder to imagine what they entailed," Marsh told him.

Kortney stirred her iced tea. "Like I said, there's a lot to it. I'll cut it short and get to how Voodoo spread from Haiti to New Orleans. It sustained the slaves through their suffering in Haiti and set the stage for a series of revolts. Between 1791 and 1804, a rebellion begun by a former slave named Françoise-Dominique Toussaint Louverture resulted in the French getting kicked out. Those who survived fled to New Orleans. Some of them brought their French-speaking slaves with them and guess what? Those slaves were Voodoo practitioners! It's as if Voodoo refused to be stamped out. I love how it shows the fierceness and stubbornness of its devotees. No matter how brutally suppressed it was the people stolen from Africa and their descendants refused to give it up. Before too long it had strong roots in New Orleans, where it was practiced by the beautiful and famous Marie Laveau." Kortney fanned herself with her hand. "Whew. And there you have it:

Voodoo 101. There's much more to it than that. That's the condensed version."

"That was very interesting. Do you think you'd be able to help us get rid of the tulpa that's been bothering us?" Aimee asked.

"You mentioned that earlier. How come you think a tulpa is bothering you?"

Aimee looked at Karen, who shrugged. "Because Karen did a foolish thing and created one," Aimee said.

"I didn't think it would turn out the way it did," Karen said defensively. "I read about tulpas and was curious to see if I could cause one to manifest. I did and it was fine at first but then it got to be creepy. I think it could be dangerous. It follows me around. When I left the monastery in Mississippi, it managed to follow me here."

"Do you see it now?" asked Kortney. She looked around the room as if the tulpa might be lurking in a corner.

"No, it's not here now. And it's not just me who's seen it. Aimee and Marsh and Trainor have seen it, too. The servants at White Oaks have seen it. It's not a hallucination; it's real. It zapped Marsh with a beam of electricity and it jumped out in front of a car we were riding in, forcing us into a ditch. I think it intends to hurt us, maybe even kill us. That's why we need help," Karen told her.

"I see," said Kortney thoughtfully. "Here's the thing, though. I'm not convinced that tulpas aren't poltergeists. I think the Bell Witch was a poltergeist, an unusual one that was able to take on different physical appearances, like funny-looking animals and one time, a girl in a green dress, swinging from a tree limb. I think Gef the talking mongoose was a poltergeist too. "

The Trapnells considered that in silence, not wanting to ask who, or what Gef the talking mongoose was.

"Does it really matter what it is? Can't you use your Voodoo powers to get rid of it?" Aimee asked.

Kortney sighed. "I don't have the power to do anything. I'd have to appeal to the right loa to intercede with Bondye and ask that whatever it is goes away and stops bothering y'all."

"So what's the big deal? Ask the right loa. Give it perfume or whatever it wants," said Trainor. He picked a cookie crumb from the front of his shirt and ate it.

"That's easier said than done," Kortney told him. "There are more than one thousand loa. They're grouped in seventeen *nanchon*, or pantheons. There's Rada loa, Petro loa and Gede loa. There's Loko, Ayizan, Damballa Wedo and Ayida-Weddo, La Sirène, and Agwé, to name a few. It would be like telling somebody who has a problem to go ask the government for help without telling them which person working in which office in which part of the government they should ask. See? It's complicated."

"So what are we supposed to do?" Aimee asked. She felt frustrated. She'd sat through a long lecture about Voodoo and now it appeared Kortney wouldn't be able to help them.

"I know it's no consolation, but if it's a poltergeist, it'll eventually go away on its own," Kortney said.

Marsh cleared his throat. "Excuse me, but from what I understand poltergeist activity is caused by the presence of a young person, usually one who's going through puberty. The word poltergeist is German, roughly meaning 'noisy ghost.' They're reported to knock on walls and throw stones and break glassware. This creature that's been bothering us doesn't do that. Then there's the issue of Karen's age. She's over sixty years old. Isn't that far too old for her to have triggered poltergeist activity? No insult intended, Karen. You're very youthful," he added gallantly.

"You're lying. I look ancient and you know it, but thanks," Karen said.

"That's true. All the poltergeist cases I've ever heard about involve an adolescent," Kortney said. She got up and selected a book from the shelf. Paging through it she said, "Here's one from Florida in the nineteen-sixties. It happened in a warehouse where they stored cheesy souvenirs like ashtrays and shot glasses and back-scratchers with palm trees and alligators on them. Boxes full of glassware got thrown off the shelves when nobody was nearby. A lot of merchandise got broken. They think the focus in that case was a nineteen-year-old warehouse worker. That's a little bit old for somebody to produce RSPK, but I guess you could consider them to still be going through adolescence. For someone Karen's age, well, I've never heard of it happening to someone her age."

"RSPK, isn't that's moving objects through the power of concentration?" said Karen. "Didn't the Russians do tests on people who could do it?"

Kortney paged through the book, looking for something. "Recurrent spontaneous psychokinesis. Yes, the Russians tested people for it. So did researchers from at least two American universities and the United States government. During the Cold War both sides tried out all sorts of things, including remote viewing, telepathy, and mind control.

She looked up and shook her head. "There was a Russian woman named Nina Kalagina who could reportedly stop a frog's heart from beating using the power of her mind. No doubt other things went on that we don't know about."

She found what she was searching for. "Here's another case. It happened in a law office in Germany in nineteen sixty-seven. A nineteen-year-old secretary was working there when all hell broke loose. The phones went crazy, dialing the automatic number for the time over and over, faster than humanly possible. Light fixtures exploded or swung wildly back and forth. A framed painting spun on its hook. A parapsychologist named Hans Bender went there and talked to the secretary. He concluded that she was unconsciously making all that happen. She didn't like her job and she and her fiancé had broken up. Bender believed that her frustration and unhappiness touched off poltergeist activity. She quit working there and it stopped. Everything went back to normal."

She closed the book and returned it to the shelf. "I work with teenagers. I can testify to the power of hormones. Perfectly nice kids hit puberty and they turn into wild animals. I've worked with kids for a long time, but I never met one yet who could break dishes with their mind. Generally, they get obsessed with sex and worry that they're not good-looking enough. It's a rough time of life. I wouldn't be a teenager again for a million dollars."

"I would. I liked being a teenager," said Trainor.

"My point is poltergeist activity is extremely rare," Kortney said. "Cases have been reported since the first century, but nobody can explain why it happens. Even though Karen is older than the usual poltergeist agent, I still think the thing y'all are calling a tulpa is a poltergeist. If it is, it'll go away on its own. Poltergeist activity always stops, eventually."

Marsh frowned. "So what do you suggest we do? Sit around and wait for it to stop? It's already menacing us. It burned me on the arm. It made Trainor drive into a ditch. What if it does something worse? How long before these poltergeists give up and go away? Days? Weeks? Months?"

Kortney bit her lip. "It depends. Usually a couple of weeks, but it could take months, even years. The Enfield poltergeist was active for about two years."

"Aw, crap! Two years?" Trainor moaned.

"It's possible."

Trainor considered that silently. Then he brightened. "Maybe we should send Karen away someplace. The cowboy thing would go with her, since it follows her. We could send her on a cruise around the world, a real nice cruise, no expense spared. Would you like that, Karen?"

Before Karen could speak, Marsh shook his head. "Absolutely not. Karen came to us for help. We are not getting rid of her in her hour of need by sending her on a cruise. Cruise ships are horrid. They're like floating ant hills, full of obnoxious drunken tourists packed in like sardines, yelling and elbowing their way to the buffet table. I'd rather be shot than go on one."

He turned to Kortney. "Isn't there anything you can do?"

"Let me think on it. I'll pray for guidance and get back to you," she said.

CHAPTER TWENTY-SIX –
TWO GUNSHOTS

Marsh and Aimee were sitting on the balcony outside Marsh's room the morning after their visit to Kortney. Marsh had assembled the rifle which had previously been in pieces on his bed. It lay across his lap.

Below them they saw Karen walk across the patio with Seamus. The dog was leaping and running in circles, excited to be outside after being cooped up indoors all night.

"Do you think Kortney will be able to do anything about the tulpa?" Aimee asked.

"I'm confident we'll be hearing from her soon," Marsh replied.

"Why?"

"Because one of the books on her bookshelves was written by good old Dorje Rinpoche, the crooked swami. The title page had a personalized message from him, warmly thanking her for attending a series of lectures he gave at his Peaceful Place monastery two months ago."

Aimee was puzzled. "Karen was staying there two months ago. She didn't say anything about seeing Kortney there."

"No, and Kortney didn't mention being there. When Karen told her she was a Buddhist nun, you'd think Kortney would have said something about being at those lectures."

"That's strange," Aimee agreed. "Do you think Karen really was at the monastery, or is she just pretending she was? Why would she lie? Or do you think she was there and so was Kortney, but they're pretending they didn't see each other there? Do you think they're hiding something?"

"It's possible. They could have concocted the tulpa story together. The rinpoche could be in on it, but I can't figure out what their motivation might be. It seems suspicious, whatever it is," Marsh raised the binoculars on the candlestick table at his side and swept his gaze across the property at the back of the house. The lush gardens bloomed peacefully in the morning sun.

Karen took a tube of sunblock from the pocket of her shorts and began applying it to her arms and legs. "Kortney seems so normal. She's a high school math teacher, for heaven's sake. Why would a math teacher be mixed up in this?"

Marsh lowered the binoculars and regarded his sister with an indulgent smile. "Professor Moriarty taught mathematics."

"That's fiction. This is reality," Aimee said. "Although, now that I think of it, Kortney's grandfather came close to bringing about the end of the world. I wonder if Kortney's secretly a criminal, like Hillman? He worked for us for sixty years, peaceful as could be, and then, with no warning, he tried to kill everyone."

"You can never tell about people," said Marsh. He picked up the binoculars again.

"You know what else I wonder? I wonder if Trainor could be involved. He's the one who suggested going to a Voodoo priestess in the first place. Do you think he's cooked up some kind of plot with Kortney? Or with Kortney and Karen? Could they all be in this together?" Aimee asked.

Marsh snorted. "Trainor's not smart enough. He couldn't come up with anything this complicated. However I wouldn't put anything past his buddy Peach Walker. Trainor is gullible enough to do whatever Peach tells him, but I don't see this – whatever this is – as being Peach's handiwork, although you never know. Let's keep an eye on Trainor, too, just in case."

Below them Karen tossed a tennis ball in the direction of the conservatories. Seamus ran after it, his tail waving.

"Karen gave Judge Sparks Daddy's will, so we're getting our inheritance. Trainor usually gets involved in Peach Walker's schemes because he needs money. Now he'll have plenty of money; we all will," Aimee said. "I wonder..."

She didn't get to finish what she was about to say because just then a figure stepped out from behind the orchid conservatory. It was the cowboy.

Marsh raised the rifle.

His first shot punched a hole in the glass and went straight through the building, shattering clay pots and sending dirt and blossoms flying. It blew out a pane of glass above the cowboy's head. His second shot was a duplicate of the first. The heavy bullets had a powder charge capable of taking down a grizzly bear and the conservatory was starting to resemble something from a war zone. There was broken glass everywhere. Mist from the artificial waterfall drifted out through the broken panes.

The cowboy took off in the direction of the swamp, with Seamus racing after him. Marsh tracked the fleeing figure in the cowboy hat with his rifle, sighting down the barrel.

"Don't!" Aimee cried. "You'll hit Seamus."

Karen was frantically calling to the dog to stop. He ignored her.

Aimee looked on in horror. What if the cowboy zapped Seamus with the bolt of electricity, the way he had Marsh? What if he killed Seamus?

"Seamus, come here! Cookie! Want a cookie?" Karen shouted.

Seamus skidded to a stop, stiff-legged, digging his feet into the turf like a calf-roping pony. He gave up his pursuit of the cowboy and trotted back toward the house, having found the lure of a dog biscuit irresistible.

Marsh lowered the rifle.

"At a hundred yards I shouldn't have missed," he said. "I'm not used to this rifle. I was expecting more of a recoil with it chambered in .30/06. At least the recoil management system works; that's good to know." He looked at the gaping holes punched into the conservatory and groaned. "That was antique glass. It will be impossible to match."

"Don't worry about the glass. What about the cowboy? He went into the swamp. You could go in after him," Aimee suggested.

"Why don't you go in after him?" Marsh asked pleasantly. "Here, take my rifle. Go on and see what happens."

Aimee gave him a hostile look.

Karen clipped Seamus' leash to his collar and looked up at the balcony. She called out, "Was that you shooting?"

"Yes," called Marsh.

"You missed him," Karen said.

"I know," Marsh replied.

"I'm going inside," called Karen.

"Come on up," called Marsh. "I've got something to tell Kortney."

"What are you going to tell her?" Aimee asked as Karen passed below them.

Marsh smiled. "You'll see. It just so happened that I had a visitation in the night."

CHAPTER TWENTY-SEVEN – OGUN

Later that day the Trapnells were assembled in the Gentlemen's Parlor along with Kortney, who was there at Marsh's invitation.

The ever-proper Lee served Arnold Palmers – iced tea and lemonade. He brought in a tray with ramekins of duck liver mousse with caramelized cipolline onions and morel mushrooms. Toast points were arranged on a bone china plate. Another plate held an assortment of crudités. For Trainor there was a peanut butter and jelly sandwich.

"I made sure Louetta cut the crusts off, sir, the way you like it," Lee told Trainor.

The sandwich had two sugar peas and a piece of strawberry fruit leather on top, forming eyes and a smiling mouth. "It's a funny face!" Trainor said delightedly.

"Indeed, it's very amusing, sir," Lee said and left the room.

Kortney held the antique photograph which Marsh had discovered, the one of the young black woman with the blacksmith and a group of male slaves. Marsh had removed it from its frame and exposed a yellowed paper label glued to the back. Written on it in faded copperplate handwriting was 'Moses and Bestie with field hands. White Oaks. June 9, 1840.'

Kortney looked at it wonderingly. "She looks like me, the way I looked thirty-odd years ago. She looks a little bit like my sister Kortnessa when we were young. We're twins, but not identical twins. This girl here could be me. She's thinner, but other than that it could be me, back when I used to rock out to Sister Sledge and Lisa Lisa."

"I noticed the resemblance," said Marsh. "Note the name Bestie. That's your grandmother's name, isn't it?"

Kortney couldn't tear her eyes away from the photograph. "It is," she murmured.

Marsh smiled kindly. "I suspect that young woman was your ancestor. She looks strong and capable, despite her life of hardship. That could be why her name was passed down through the generations, as a way of honoring her."

Kortney blotted her eyes with a cocktail napkin and laughed ruefully. "Oh, dear, I'm happy and sad at the same time. I'm happy to see her face, but I'm sad because, well, you know."

"I'm sorry that my family played a role in her unhappiness, and the unhappiness of others. Please keep the photograph. Before too long I hope to be able to do something more substantial as a form of reparation. It can never be enough, but I intend to do what I can," Marsh told her.

"Thank you. I'll treasure this," Kortney said. She placed the photograph carefully in her purse.

Marsh selected a stalk of blanched asparagus from among the crudités and sprinkled it with sea salt. "I have something to discuss with you. I already told my brother and sisters about it. We don't know what to make of it. We thought perhaps you might." He shook his head and frowned. "I still can't believe it," he murmured. "Nothing like it ever happened to me before."

Trainor piped up. "Tell her, Marsh."

Marsh crossed his legs and neatened the crease in his trousers. "All right. Perhaps the photograph had something to do with it. I went to bed last night, thinking about it. For some reason my thoughts kept returning to the blacksmith, the tall, heavily muscled man named Moses. I must have fallen asleep, because the next thing I knew I was standing near a huge stone fireplace filled with coals and leaping flames. I could smell the smoke from the fire and feel its intense heat, that's how real it seemed. Sparks flew as a giant of a man used a hammer to beat on a piece of metal on top of an andiron."

Marsh regarded them with wide eyes. "It felt *real,* as if it were actually happening. This man, this blacksmith, had to be at least eight feet tall. He had a dog by his side. He was swinging his hammer, fashioning something metal, a machete or a sword, I couldn't tell which. He turned to me and in a voice like thunder he intoned, 'I am Hogan. Like you I am a warrior. I will assist you with your problem. In return I want red meat. I want pomegranates, grapes, and rum. I want alligator peppers. Bring me these things.' Then he struck the andiron with his mallet, making a sound like a great bell. A wall of flames and smoke rose up. I flinched and closed my eyes. When I opened them he was gone. I was alone in my room, wide-awake in bed. What do you think of that?"

"That's a freaky dream, all right," Trainor said.

Marsh was watching Kortney. "What do you think, Kortney?"

She looked at him appraisingly. "He was a black man?"

"Yes, he was very dark skinned and he was enormous, like an offensive lineman."

"He said his name was Hogan?"

"It sounded like Hogan," Marsh said.

"Could it have been Ogun?" she asked.

"Perhaps. Why?"

"Because that's the name of a loa. He's often represented as working with metal. Do you remember what he was wearing?"

Marsh looked up at the ceiling, his lips pressed together. "He was bare-chested. He might have had on a kilt, or a sarong. I don't remember, but I remember he had something bright red tied around his waist, a sash, I think."

"You're describing Ogun," Kortney told him.

"Really? I never heard of him. What do you suppose it means? Is it some sort of sign?" Marsh asked.

Kortney studied him. "It really happened the way you said? You're not saying it to make fun of me because I told you I practice Voodoo?"

"Kortney, I swear I would never make fun of you," said Marsh.

She grew excited. "Then you had a visitation from Ogun. It makes sense, you being involved in the arms trade. Ogun is the spirit of iron tools, war and weapons, among other things. My goodness, this is extraordinary!"

"It certainly is," said Marsh.

"He asked you for stuff," Trainor reminded him.

"That's right, red meat, rum, pomegranates and so on. Are those traditional offerings to Ogun?" Marsh asked Kortney. He knew very well that they were. He'd done some research online to make his imaginary dream sound more convincing.

"Those are some of them, as well as knives and guns," said Kortney.

"That's no problem; Marsh has plenty of guns. So what do we do? Do we get all that stuff together? Then what? You conjure him up?" Trainor asked Kortney.

She spread mousse on a toast point, frowning. "I would perform a ceremony where an offering was made to Ogun. If he wishes he would help you get rid of your troublesome visitor, tulpa or poltergeist or whatever it is. He would possess the body of a supplicant and speak through him. That's if he chooses to appear. It's not guaranteed."

"When could you do it?" Karen asked.

"In the next couple of days. I need to make sure nobody's using the place where I'd do it. Marsh, you should gather the things Ogun asked you for. Better get some catfish fillets, too. As long as we're going out there we might as well have a fish fry. We can include catfish in the offering. Ogun is well-disposed toward a nice piece of catfish."

"Going out where?" asked Aimee.

"Out to Revenuer's Sorrow," Kortney said.

CHAPTER TWENTY-EIGHT –
REVENUER'S SORROW

Water sparkled in a pond fringed with cattails. Every so often a fish or a frog broke the surface with a splash. A boat ramp led to a wooden dock. In the middle of the pond was a fiberglass swim platform equipped with a slide and diving board.

A fenced-in playground area held slides and swings and monkey bars. There was a horseshoe pit and a volleyball net. A prefabricated building housed changing rooms and a pair of chemical toilets.

Beneath a tin-roofed pavilion were several picnic tables. Kortney, Marsh, Aimee and Karen were seated at one of the tables. Trainor was occupied in cooking catfish fillets on an impressively large gas grill. He was drinking a bottle of beer and wore a straw sombrero and a barbecue apron with GRILL SERGEANT on it.

It might have been a small but well-equipped summer camp, except for one thing. In a nearby meadow was a stone grotto. In the center was a wooden pole painted with bright colors in a design of two intertwined serpents.

"I never realized all this was back here," Aimee said.

Kortney took a drink of her iced tea. On the cement floor beside her was a box containing a top hat and a cigar. Earlier she'd explained to the Trapnells what she intended to do with them.

"Paw-Paw Hilly and his brothers and sisters clubbed in to buy it from Gordon Buzzy's daddy, sometime in the late sixties or early seventies," she said. "All this land used to belong to the Buzzys. Paw-Paw Hilly and my great-uncles cleared it themselves, using chainsaws. They sold the lumber and made it into a family gathering place. My nephews come out here to ride dirt bikes."

"How come it's called Revenuer's Sorrow?" Karen asked.

Kortney smiled. "That's a funny story. It used to be called Buzzy's Woods. The Buzzy men were moonshiners. They had stills hidden in the woods all over, including one right around where we are now."

She swatted at a mosquito. "How's that catfish coming along?" she called out to Trainor.

"Just about done," he called back.

"I suspect it's too done. You shouldn't overcook catfish. It's a rookie mistake," Kortney confided to the others. "Anyway, getting back to how this place got its name, the alcohol tax people got word that the Buzzys were brewing 'shine. Back in the days of Prohibition folks who went around busting up stills and arresting moonshiners were called revenuers. The name stuck after Prohibition was repealed. This one particular revenuer heard the Buzzys had a still back here. This would have been right before World War II. One moonless night he drove along the dirt roads and through the piney woods until he came out to a clearing by that pond over there." She motioned toward the pond and they turned to look, picturing the scene.

"The story goes that he was driving his personal vehicle, a brand-new midnight-blue Cadillac with red leather upholstery and whitewall tires. He was mighty proud of that Caddy. The revenuer parked and got out. He crept through the woods, being stealthy, trying to see if he could spot the Buzzys tending their still. That's when he heard a tremendous explosion. It was his car, the pride and joy of his life. Somebody blew it up with dynamite. They never did find out who it was. The Buzzys were the prime suspects, but they had alibis. They claimed to have been at a revival meeting over in Pontahatcha, getting saved. Several people swore they saw them there and nobody could prove any different. That's how this place came to be called Revenuer's Sorrow."

"Fish is ready. Come and get it," called Trainor

They ate grilled catfish and coleslaw and potato salad, glancing every so often at the grotto in the meadow. Marsh had brought along a cooler. It formerly held the catfish fillets and now contained the reminder of his morning shopping trip: four sirloin steaks wrapped in butcher paper resting on a bed of ice. The steaks were intended as an offering to Papa Legba, gatekeeper to the spirit world. When the time came Kortney planned to put on the top hat, light the cigar and attempt to summon him. A bottle of Bougainville Vieux Domaine spiced rum was on the picnic table, its seal unbroken. That was for Papa Legba, too.

"I wonder where the tulpa is?" asked Aimee.

"I hope it shows up," Marsh said. "Ogun could squash that tulpa like a grape. I wouldn't mind watching two supernatural entities have a showdown."

Kortney gave him a severe look. "This is not a laughing matter."

"I apologize," Marsh said. "Oh, look. Someone's coming."

A black Mercedes SUV with black-tinted windows slowly rolled down the narrow driveway, its tires crunching on the gravel.

Kortney stood up and studied the vehicle over the top of her sunglasses. "That can't be any of my relatives. I told them to stay away. I wonder who it is? This is posted as private property."

"I suspect it's Dorje Rinpoche. I invited him," Marsh said.

"You did what?" said Karen.

"I invited him," Marsh repeated calmly. "I always wanted to meet a holy man who used to be in cahoots with the CIA. I'll bet he has loads of interesting stories to tell about the good old days back in Nepal when he was running drugs and intimidating witnesses."

"You didn't tell me you were inviting anybody. I wouldn't have given permission. Damn it, Marsh. That's it. It's off. I'm not doing this," Kortney picked up the cardboard box. "Good luck getting rid of that tulpa or poltergeist or whatever it is. I hope it sticks around and bothers y'all for years. It would serve y'all right."

"I didn't do anything," Aimee said. "Why should I have to suffer? Go ahead and be mad at Marsh if you want to, but can't you stay and do your ceremony?"

"I didn't do nothing neither," said Trainor. "Is that the head guy from your monastery, Karen?"

The man who got out of the Mercedes was young and white. He resembled a fatter version of Justin Bieber.

"That's not the rinpoche, that's his assistant, Richard Einsinger. He takes care of the rinpoche's correspondence and drives him places." Karen craned her neck. "That's strange, the rinpoche's not with him."

"There goes my theory," said Marsh. "It appears Dorje Rinpoche isn't behind this after all, unless he sent this fellow to do his dirty work for him."

Einsinger approached them. He had a gun in his hand. "Nobody move," he shouted. "Put your hands in the air."

"Ugh, how depressing. He's wearing those dreadful plastic sandals with holes in them. I prefer my adversaries to be better shod," said Marsh. He raised his hands and the others followed suit.

"On your feet," Einsinger ordered. "Turn your pockets inside-out. Put everything on the table. If any of you are armed put your gun on the table. I'm going to pat you down. If I find you had a gun and you didn't put it on the table, I'll be very upset."

They turned out their pockets, removing keys and wallets and cell phones and placing them on the table. Marsh removed his Glock from its pancake holster and put it on the table. Einsinger picked it up, ejected the magazine and threw it into the pond. He pocketed the gun and proceeded to pat them down.

"I see you've got a CZ P-09," said Marsh conversationally, nodding at the gun in Einsinger's hand. "It holds twenty rounds of ammunition. Is that because you intend to shoot all five of us without having to stop to reload? That's mass murder. You can get into considerable trouble for that. Georgia has capital punishment. They take it quite seriously. People are executed all the time up at the death house in Atlanta."

Einginger gave him a surly look. "Shut your cake hole, Shrimpy Jim, or I'll shut it for you."

"Where's Dorje Rinpoche? You didn't do anything to him, did you?" asked Karen.

"He's at the monastery. I didn't do anything to him, not yet. Which one of you sent the email from BangBang78?"

"That would be me, aka Shrimpy Jim," said Marsh.

Einsinger smirked. "Thanks for the heads-up, smartass. I deleted it before the rinpoche saw it. He doesn't know I'm here. He probably thinks I'm out picking up his dry cleaning and running errands for him and the rest of the dumbasses at that stupid monastery."

"What's this all about?" asked Aimee.

"You should sing that." In a falsetto voice Einsinger warbled, "What's it all about, Richard?" He chortled and slapped his jeans-clad thigh.

"Oh, dear. He's not only armed he's insane," said Marsh.

"Say that again and I'll shoot you in the knee," Einsinger snarled.

"I promise I won't say it again. Please tell us, what is going on?"

"What's going on is you're a bunch of idiots. Her, over there, the old chick, she thinks she created a tulpa, the dumb bitch," said Einsinger, pointing to Karen.

"I take it she didn't?" said Marsh.

"Of course not, but all the dumbasses at the monastery think she did. She babbled to everybody about how she was trying to create a tulpa. She never shut up about it. They encouraged her. That's because they've got their heads up their asses with all that Buddhist bullshit," Einsinger said derisively.

"You're not a Buddhist?" Trainor said.

"Hardly. Do I look like a dumbass? The old chick is going to inherit billions. She signed it over to the rinpoche so he can buy more statues and gongs and shit for his dumbass Peaceful Place. I'm the rinpoche's adopted son. He adopted me last year after I convinced him I was his son in another life, which shows what a moron he is. When he dies, I'll inherit half of his estate. The other half goes to the temple. I'm going to make sure he dies sooner rather than later," Einsinger said.

"If I didn't create a tulpa, who did?" Karen asked.

"Jesus Christ in a bounce house, you really don't get it, do you? Nobody created him, unless it was his mom and dad. He's not a tulpa, he's a guy. Hey, Charlie, come on out!"

The side door to the SUV slid open. A familiar grinning figure in a cowboy costume stepped out. "Howdy, folks," he said.

"Meet my friend Charlie. He's an acrobat and an illusionist," said Einsinger.

"Well, dang!" said Trainor. "Guess the Voodoo ceremony ain't gonna work."

CHAPTER TWENTY-NINE – THE POTOMITAN CLAIMS A VICTIM

"Is that what you're doing out here, a Voodoo ceremony? The email just said it was important for the rinpoche to come out here, and gave the GPS coordinates," said Einsinger. "Is that what the top hat and the cigar were for or were y'all planning on having yourselves a costume party?" He laughed nastily.

"They were for summoning Papa Legba, along with the rum and the steaks," said Kortney.

Einsinger looked at them in disbelief. "You people are crazy. First Buddhism and now Voodoo. They're not real. They were made up by primitive savages."

"I take it you're not a religious man," Marsh said.

"I favor the Viking religion," said Einsinger.

Charlie the erstwhile tulpa spoke up. "What's that little stone hut over there?"

Marsh looked uncomfortable. "That's a sacred space. I ask you not to go in there and tamper with the offerings."

Einsinger narrowed his eyes. "Why not? What offerings?"

"I told you, it's a sacred space. The grapes and pomegranates and gold coins and precious gems and other things are intended as an offering. Please don't disturb it."

"Gold coins, eh? Precious gems? I think I will go and disturb it, how about that? In fact I think I'll help myself to it. How do you like that, smart guy?" Einsinger started in the direction of the grotto. "Keep an eye on them," he told Charlie. "If any of them moves zap them with the stun gun."

Charlie unclipped an object from his belt.

"He *does* have a stun gun, a small one that can be easily concealed. That solves that mystery," said Marsh.

Einsinger had reached the grotto. He stood looking at it, shaking his head in disgust. "Some nut built this and put in a pole with snakes painted on it. That's the weirdest thing I ever saw." He stepped up and onto the wooden floorboards. "I don't see any gold coins or gems, just a lot of fruit," he called out. "Were you shitting me?"

"Get closer to the pole. They're there," said Marsh.

Einsinger stepped closer to the decorated pole in the center of the small building. As he leaned down to examine the objects on the floor, the heavy pole broke free of its masonry pedestal. It toppled, hitting him on the head and knocking him out. The gun flew out of his hand and sailed through the air, landing in a dense tangle of cogongrass and tropical spiderwort.

"The loa have spoken," said Marsh with satisfaction.

Kortney stared at him, open-mouthed. "Did you rig that to happen?"

"No, I had nothing to do with it," he said. "I had hoped he'd be distracted searching for the nonexistent gold coins and precious gems and I could rush him. It would be a risk, but he wouldn't be able to shoot all five of us, not if the rest of you scattered. Some of you would probably escape. Keep that in mind if you're ever in a group that's confronted by a single gunman."

Charlie was backing away from them, toward the SUV.

"Don't leave now; the fun's just starting," Marsh told him, moving toward the horseshoe pit.

"Stay away from me," cried Charlie. He looked into the SUV. "Dammit, Richard's got the keys." He began walking backward, up the driveway and toward the two-lane county road at the end. "Stay back," he warned them, brandishing the stun gun.

Marsh bent and picked up an object lying in the sand of the horseshoe pit. He hefted it, preparing to throw it.

"You can't throw a horseshoe far enough to hit me from there. Even if you did, it wouldn't hurt me much," Charlie shouted.

"How about a boomerang? Would that hurt you much?" Lightning fast, Marsh whipped the boomerang at him. It whizzed through the air, striking him in the head with a loud *klonk!* Charlie's feet flew out from under him and he collapsed.

Marsh went over and crouched beside Einsinger. He shook his head. "His skull is crushed. He appears to be dead. We'd better call an ambulance, in case he's still alive. His associate may be alive, although a hunting boomerang packs quite a punch. Men have been killed by them. At the very least he'll have a nasty headache."

"Why didn't it come back? I thought boomerangs were supposed to come back," said Trainor.

"Not all of them. That one was a non-returning boomerang. Aboriginal Australians sometimes use them for hunting game," Marsh said. Kortney was staring at the two bodies in horror. He told her, "You might want to have a word with your nephews, if they're the ones who brought the boomerang out here. It's not a toy."

"Oh, I will, don't you worry," she said.

Aimee was on her phone, calling for an ambulance. "It's about three miles outside of Cobbs, off County Road 56, at Revenuer's Sorrow," she told the dispatcher. "There's two men with head injuries. You'd better send the sheriff, too. Tell him Ms. von Helgren wants him. Tell him we caught the tulpa. He'll know what that means." She ended the call.

Marsh sat down at the picnic table and opened the bottle of rum. "Anyone care for a drink? Papa Legba won't be needing this, although..." He picked up the bottle and carried it to the grotto. Avoiding Einsinger's sprawled body he approached the toppled pole. He poured some rum onto the broken masonry pedestal. "Thank you," he murmured.

"I don't understand it. My Uncle Claude built me that *hounfour*. He was a master mason. Things Uncle Claude built stayed built. That pedestal anchoring the potomitan was called a *socle*. It was as strong as the Rock of Ages. Nothing should have made it collapse, except maybe an earthquake," Kortney said.

"And yet it did," said Marsh. He poured an ounce of rum into a plastic glass and tossed it back.

CHAPTER THIRTY – EWELL HASKINS GETS HIS REWARD

With the exception of his wedding day and the birth of his children it was the best day of Sheriff Ewell Haskins' entire life. He'd been to the country club before, to attend various events as a guest of one of the members, but this time he himself was a member, having been nominated for membership by none other than Marsh Trapnell. He could hardly believe it. He kept taking the membership card out of his wallet in secret and looking at it, scarcely crediting its reality. He, Ewell Elbert Haskins, had finally arrived. The card proved it. He was officially a member of the upper class, at least as far as such things were reckoned in Cobbs, Georgia.

He held his wife's hand and conducted her into the club's dining room as if he were ushering her through the gates of paradise.

"They got all your favorites, darlin'. They got club sandwiches and shrimp cocktails and Waldorf salad. If you want somethin' that's not on the menu just ask Bernard. He's the head waiter. He'll tell them to make it for you," he told her proudly.

Cressilda Haskins squeezed his hand. She wore a dress she'd bought especially for the occasion. It was candy apple red, made of organdy, with a skirt like a tutu and what was called a sweetheart neckline. She'd sprayed on twice as much Joie de Passion cologne as usual. Ewell could feel her hand trembling in his.

"It's so sophisticated and elegant," she said in a hushed voice, looking around at the faux walnut paneling and the dusty swag curtains on the windows overlooking the nine-hole golf course.

"It sure is," her husband said proudly. "Sometimes, when they're putting on a big wing-ding, they have an ice sculpture and a chocolate fountain and as much shrimp and crab legs as you can eat."

"Oh, my goodness! It'll be like being on a cruise, except we get to stay right here in Cobbs and not have to meet foreigners," Cressilda said delightedly.

Marsh approached them. As usual he was impeccably dressed. He wore a cream-colored cable-knit sweater over a pink and white striped cotton shirt. Madras check trousers, a vintage Longines stainless steel watch and python skin loafers completed his outfit.

Cressilda, who regarded him and all of the Trapnells with mingled awe and apprehension, suppressed an urge to curtsy. The usually reserved Marsh surprised her by taking both her hands in his and speaking warmly to her.

"It's lovely to see you, Cressilda. You're like a breath of fresh air in this musty old place. I am certain the ladies will appreciate your participation in their various activities. The winter cotillion will be coming up and I know for a fact that they will look to you for ideas about a theme and decorations." He smiled at her and she felt herself blush.

"I'll be glad to help however I can," she said.

Marsh turned to Ewell Haskins. "Thank you, Sheriff, for keeping me informed on the progress of that fellow I hit with the boomerang."

"He's gonna need a steel plate put in his head, but they think he'll recover. Then he can be tried for assault and menacing and attempted larceny and maybe attempted murder. The prosecutor's still working out the details," Haskins said, adding, "Good thing the other fellow's dead. That saves us the trouble of a trial."

"I shall appreciate being kept informed," said Marsh. "As you know, Charlie Esposito and his partner, Richard Einsinger, the rinpoche's adopted son, fooled my stepsister Karen into thinking she created a supernatural being called a tulpa. They got away with it by Einsinger having an intimate knowledge of the layout of the Peaceful Place monastery. Esposito was a skilled illusionist. He could whisk into cupboards and cubbyholes while appearing to vanish. I would have thought someone would have been able to get close enough to him to grab him, but my stepsister said he always stayed just out of reach. There was also the belief that touching him would cause harm to her, in the same way that touching a spirit conjured by a physical medium was thought to cause harm to the medium."

"I don't hold with any of that supernatural mumbo-jumbo," said Haskins, who happened to be mortally afraid of ghosts.

"You are sagacious," said Marsh. "I must confess that I am open-minded on the subject."

"What I don't understand is how Esposito got from Natchez to Cobbs. It's five hundred miles, one-way," said Haskins.

"That's easy; Einsinger drove him here and dropped him off. Charlie Esposito camped in the woods behind the fertilizer plant, making forays to White Oaks in order to intimidate us. Nobody likes to go near the fertilizer plant unless they absolutely have to because of the way it smells. The factory foreman found a tent and a sleeping bag and some supplies back there. It couldn't have been a pleasant camping spot, but Esposito was willing to put up with it for the sake a large payoff if everything went according to plan. A supposed tulpa can't very well check into the nearest motel, not when a skilled law enforcement officer such as yourself would know to canvass the local motels when told of a suspicious-acting stranger," Marsh said.

"That's right," said Haskins, who had thought of no such thing.

"Initially I thought Dorje Rinpoche was behind this, but he had nothing to do with it. It came as a surprise to him that his adopted son had engineered an elaborate plot and was planning to kill him in order to obtain the money my stepsister had pledged to the monastery. I met with him. He's a charming gentleman. Apparently in his case a leopard was able to change its spots. I'm convinced he really did give up a life a crime in order to seek enlightenment. Perhaps someday I'll be able to spend more time with him. I think there is much that he could teach me."

Marsh bowed. "And now I must leave you. My family will be spending Thanksgiving in Manhattan, with my sister's son and her snakes. I wish you both a happy holiday."

He turned and left the room. Cressilda and Ewell Haskins watched him go. "Manhattan," whispered Cressilda. "That's the same as New York City, isn't it?"

"I think so," her husband replied.

"Well, they can keep their old Manhattan and their old snakes and good luck to them. I'm happy to stay right here in Cobbs," Cressilda said.

"Me too, darlin'," her husband replied.

THE END

NOTE FROM THE AUTHOR

Word-of-mouth is crucial for any author to succeed. If you enjoyed *Black Willows*, please leave a review online—anywhere you are able. Even if it's just a sentence or two. It would make all the difference and would be very much appreciated.

Thanks!
Jill

ABOUT THE AUTHOR

Jill Hand is a former crime reporter. She is a member of *International Thriller Writers*. *White Oaks*, the first book in her series about the scheming, free-wheeling Trapnell siblings, won first place for thrillers in the 2019 PenCraft Awards. Her short stories have appeared in many anthologies.

Thank you so much for reading one of Jill Hand's novels.
If you enjoyed the experience, please check out our recommended
title for your next great read!

White Oaks by Jill Hand

"An ingeniously dark comic thriller about greed, gluttony and
murder that is destined for the big screen."
–BEST THRILLERS